THE KI

AN ORIGINAL MYSTERY NOVEL

THE KILLING MOOD

AN ORIGINAL MYSTERY NOVEL

BY

ROBERT LOUDEN

Bookstand Publishing

www.bookstandpublishing.com

Published by
Bookstand Publishing
Morgan Hill, CA 95037
3086_9

ISBN 978-1-58909-692-9

Printed in the United States of America

ACKNOWLEDGEMENTS

My many thanks to Esther for all her hard work in helping me compile this my first literary effort.

Also an extra special ‘atta girl to my very beautiful talented daughter and best friend Emma who survived the telling of “The Killing Mood”.

Sincerely,

Robert Paul Louden

CHAPTER 1

It was an early September Sunday evening, a beautiful Indian summer time of the year when Mother Nature decides to hibernate. She changes one colorful mask for another, lush green and sharp crispy browns that live on her countless variety of trees and shrubs become unlimited blends of red, yellow and even an occasional outrageous blue. Add this all together and you get the sum total of heaven on earth, the perfect season for living life on the Eastern Seaboard; Queens, New York to be exact.

Corona was just one of the many towns incorporated within Queens which was one-fifth of the boroughs that shaped the unique skyline of the great city all the world called New York. It was predominantly Italian in its makeup. Most of its families were second and third generation Americans.

On this wonderful evening one such family had just sat down to dinner. The cook was also the patriarch of this lineage and this was his home and had been for nearly forty years. He was veteran N.Y.P.D. top cop, Dominic Pisa. But before we get ahead of things, how about a little history of the man himself?

If one could describe Dominic in a single phrase, he would be the kind of man young men desire to be like growing up and what old men wish to God they had been.

Coming home from Vietnam a seasoned 25-year-old, 0300 combat Marine who had fought deep within the shit in some of the most vicious battles of an unpopular war. Back home the press with their strong liberal slant and bleeding hearts were telling our fighting boys and girls what they were doing in Southeast Asia was wrong, very wrong. How the hell do you convince soldiers willing to risk their young lives and limbs for whatever cause that they are fools, questioned Dominic.

Wearing a uniform in 1969, especially that of a Marine, was considered a kind of taboo. It was common knowledge the Corp was responsible for the lion's share of killing Vietcong, the North Vietnamese regulars as well, and even a large civilian collateral damage body count; the latter being unavoidable in any ongoing fire fight. How do you tell the loved ones of those heroes who came back in flag-draped coffins that the joke was on them?

Dominic was just one of the many confused and certainly disillusioned vets. Moving on with his high school diploma and an honorable discharge in hand. He applied for the New York City Police Department and was accepted. All of his young life he believed in doing the right thing. Here once again was a chance to help the little guy who couldn't help himself to protect and serve.

Dominic to this day is still considered old school, not too tall and not too short, just average in stature. But that's where it all ends. Not even as a rookie cop was he anything but average. An expert shot with great instincts when it came to assigning guilt. He could smell it all out before anyone else, a born investigator with tunnel vision. Once he locked onto a suspect it was like being bitten hard by a pit bull terrier. He never let up until that person or persons responsible were doing their fair share of time as guests of New Your State's finest maximum security lockups!

Sharing Dominic's meal that night were his son, Jerry, his wife, Chris, and their lovely young daughter, Maria. Dominic's dark brown eyes followed around the table as he focused on the one single empty chair that would signify repeatedly the pain and loss he and everyone present deeply felt.

Sophia Pisa was not Sicilian like her husband, Dominic. She came to America from Calabria, Italy. She was considered to be Calabrese, a light-skinned beauty with unbelievable piercing green eyes. She was multilingual, not unusual for that part of the world. However, English was not on the list. When she met Dominic Pisa quite by accident at a Catholic Knights of Columbus dance down in the Village, she was relieved he spoke her primary language, Italian, with only a slight accent. She was the girl he would always dream of meeting as though they were predestined. She was to become the softer side to his hard barked exterior. Sophia could accept him and his bullish Sicilian manner. In the still and quiet moments they were together, mostly at night in the small hours of the morning, she could reach his gentle side deep down, that which had nearly been beaten out through years of service both as a Marine and as a police officer. She was his rock. She kept it all together even to the end.

They were married for three decades plus five. A perfect fit. Happiness few men ever see in a lifetime. When she died that rainy fall day one year ago to this date, a large part of this man left as well. God giveth and God taketh away, he cried. One thing is for certain, he would repeat over and over, "I'll never stop loving her or stop loving those days I loved her."

"Dad! Are you okay? Asked Chris, Dominic's daughter-in-law.

"Sorry guys," said Dominic. "I was just somewhere else."

"We all miss her," said Jerry, looking about, "A lot of special memories here."

Jerry's remark triggered still more. Dominic could not help stop remembering things as he stared at his handsome young son.

To a Sicilian man the birth of a son was nearly equal to that of the second coming of Jesus Christ our Lord. The male heir was destined to pass on the family name, hopefully with honor and respect.

Gerald Michael Pisa came into this world not at all in an easy manner. He would suffer, in medical terms, fetal distress. He was literally being strangled by his own umbilical cord or lifeline. The delivering physician was a brilliant, young, red-headed, fair-skinned, freckled-faced Mick doctor fresh from his residency. There is only one course of action he explained to Dominic. We must go in immediately by way of cesarian section. The baby and your wife are both at high risk. Dominic agreed.

Within minutes a nurse would bring Jerry out to his troubled father, handing over his newborn. "Congratulations, Mr. Pisa," she said. "You now have a 6-pound 5-ounce, beautiful, healthy baby boy, a little worse for the wear. He was having quite a rough time of it in there but this little guy of yours had an incredible will to see the light of day and what life has to offer."

"Can I see my wife?" he asked.

"That will be a while," answered the nurse. "Dr. Regan is finishing up. He'll be out in about an hour. Don't you worry sir, she is in marvelous hands. He may be young," she said, "but he has real surgical gifts.

"Thank you nurse," said Dominic.

"Surely, now may I take your baby?" she asked. "We want to warm him up."

Dominic was amazed staring down at his co-creation while holding this brand new life for the very first time. Unless you have been there and done that, you will never ever know that strange feeling of God's presence along with his quiet instructions. This is my gift to you and your loving wife. Please do your best to love and guide him along his journey and I will do the same, cautioned the Lord.

"Look at the hair on that kid," said Dominic, passing Jerry back to the nurse. "My side of the family, thick, dark and bushy," he announced. "My wife is the pretty one, she's got most of the looks in our crowd."

After what seemed an eternity to Dominic, Dr. Reagan reappeared. "We're out of the woods," he said. "She is very weak and has lost a lot of blood. I gave her something for the pain. She'll sleep for quite a while. Why don't you go home and get some rest as well sir?" The young doctor took a beat.

Dominic read his concerned look immediately. "What is it doc?" asked Dominic. "Give me the bad news, I'm a cop. I deal day in and day out with nothing but bad things."

"Your wife has suffered internal bleeding," said the doctor. "I had to remove both her ovaries. I simply had no choice. They were infected beyond repair."

Dominic was devastated. "No more children?" he asked.

"I'm so sorry," said the doctor. "It isn't fair, I know. Life sometimes gets a bit messy as you well know, Mr.

Pisa, in your profession. But bottom line, anytime I can save one life, let alone two, I've had a great day."

"Thank you, doctor," said Dominic, while shaking his hand, "and chin-don."

"The surgeon looked a bit puzzled.

"May you live one hundred years. It's an old Italian blessing doc," said Dominic.

"Well thank you for that, Mr. Pisa."

"No, thank you young man," said Dominic.

Growing up an only child in Corona Queens wasn't easy but Jerry Pisa had a great deal of help from his friends whose last names also ended in vowels. On occasion a few of the Irish kids strayed over from their turf known as Sunny Side, perhaps in search of a genuine slice of pizza pie. Then it could get a bit ugly. All of this behavior went away when everyone was old enough to go off on their own.

Jerry idolized his dad early on. This only became stronger as Dominic's legend as a police officer grew. He loved and certainly respected his mother, who never forgot her old world roots. She taught her rugged son to respect all people regardless of race, creed or color. We were, in fact, all immigrants at one time or another. Even I, she would explain, came to Ellis Island years ago as a teenager without knowledge of English. I would learn this difficult language mostly from my young husband, your father, who was born in America. She would tell Jerry wonderful stories of both Calabria, Italy and of her newly adopted homeland, the United States.

After graduation from Junior College, earning an AA Degree in Business with a minor in Police Science, Jerry's dream had secretly been to join the force and follow in his father's, now famous footsteps, against his mother's wishes. Sophia Pisa cared too much about the dangers that surrounded her husband's career and now her only beloved son was signing on as well. She had hoped Jerry would seek out a more cautious occupation. Mom was out-voted 2 to 1. Now she would be resigned forever to worry twice as much.

The years receded by happily and without incidence. Jerry would later on meet and marry a fellow officer's beautiful Irish cousin, Chris O'Donnell. Jerry would at times tease his young bride. "I could swear you were one of those little, skinny, Irish brats my buddies and I tossed water balloons on when we were all just kids."

Their marriage would be blessed with an only child as well, a lovely newborn girl, Maria Sophia Pisa. Her middle name would honor her still beautiful and always special grandmother. Life had almost come full circle. Chris O'Donnell's parents sadly had lost their lives in a senseless and tragic automobile accident at the hands of a habitual drunken driver, who just happened to survive. Go figure. She was just entering her senior year in high school, the saddest thing of time and men are those wonderful moments that might have been.

Dinner had just completed. Jerry's wife, Chris, was helping to clear things up before she and her husband were off on a much needed holiday and some serious alone time. What could be more perfect for young people in love than to spend five romantic days and nights in a picturesque hideaway, Barbados?

"That was great, Dad," said Chris. "You couldn't get a better meal down on Mulberry Street at any price."

"Thanks, Chris," said Dominic. "My mother always stressed we kids should cook; that way we never starved. I wish I could have enjoyed it as much as you. I just wasn't very hungry."

"I wonder why you didn't teach your son here a few tricks," she said while rubbing Jerry's broad, muscular shoulders.

"Dad," he said, "it isn't enough my being a second-generation cop and I protect our mean streets, must I do it all?"

Dominic caught in the middle just shrugged.

"Sweetheart," said Chris, "you do just fine."

"Flattery, baby," replied Jerry, "will get you."

"Both late for your plane if you two don't get the lead out," said Dominic interrupting.

"We really appreciate your watching our beautiful Maria, Pop," said Jerry. "Chris and I needed a break."

"Never a problem, son," said Dominic. "You guys are all the blood I got left, we gotta take care of each other."

Jerry reached in, hugging and kissing his father in the best traditional Italian way. "And you better take better care of you! Slow down, Pop," said Jerry. "You're too old to be chasing bad guys, especially the ones that threaten you openly in public."

"Joco?" asked Dominic.

"None other," answered Jerry.

"You worry too much kid," said Dominic. "You know Chris, your husband here is just like his gorgeous, sainted mother. She always worried too. Sophia said I was a carrier, that I gave people around me ulcers. Ha!"

"I mean it," said Jerry. "Promise me you'll watch your ass."

"And you watch your mouth," warned Dominic.

"Are you sure about this?" asked Chris.

"Get out of here!" replied Dominic. "Maria and I will do just fine. Right honey?" Maria gave her grandfather a huge thumbs up. "Now have fun and don't give us another thought."

They all adjourned to the front lawn where Jerry, along with his childhood friends, engaged in flag football or some other form of combat. Steve Paisano lived just two doors down and they were inseparable growing up. Jennie Pagano lived directly across the street. She was his first gal, first kiss, first everything. A whole lot went down in that neighborhood.

Jerry's car had a flat tire. "I don't believe this!" said Jerry, "Chris, hold my jacket will you, honey?"

"No, take mine or you'll never make it," said Dominic, tossing his keys at his son.

"Are you sure?" asked Jerry.

"I'm sure. Now get going," said Dominic.

They threw their bags into Dominic's vintage Ford trunk and started the car. As they backed down the driveway that Jerry had driven over a hundred times, Chris and Jerry expressed thanks and love for both Dominic and their 6-year-old daughter. "We love you, too," said Dominic, waving goodbye while holding Maria. The car got about twenty yards away when suddenly, and without warning, it exploded into a fiery inferno. Dominic's horrified reaction was coupled with Maria's uncontrollable screaming.

CHAPTER 2

It was a cold and rainy night some three years later. A white limousine approached a very large, impeccably manicured home located in a wealthy section of Los Angeles, California known as Holmby Hills. This area is wedged in between two other equally rich and prosperous regions, Bel Air to the west and Beverly Hills just to the east. Inside the house were several men waiting to kill time, seven of these equally dangerous types were crowded around a large oval table. A high-stakes poker game was in progress. A first man, the dealer, was about to pass around to each player a second card face up. "Pair of tens, big help," he said. "Queen, ten, possible straight, queen, six, no help, and Jack, three, help!" he joked. They all shared a laugh except one. A fourth player said, "Just give me the fucking cards! I'll do the rest," he barked.

The first man dealing again replied, pointing to the man directly to his left, "Pair of tens bet."

"I'll bet a thousand," said the pair of tens.

They checked around to the fourth player, still pissed, "I'll see that and raise two thousand, bitch!

The white limousine had no sooner passed through the giant security gates and up the circular drive to the front door of serious money when the lone figure of Frank Pansine observing the car through rain-soaked windows remarked. "Who'd a thought that nigger, Joco, would come out in this shit," he said.

Johnny Brandoli, a handsome card player, spoke up, “We’ve got more clean money in here than he can count, Mr. Pansine, Joco couldn’t pass!”

Back down the block there was another shiny car parked in the shadows. Through its steamy windshield sat Police Lieutenant Dominic Pisa and his black partner, Charley Sawyer, drinking cold, stale coffee and listening to the conversations emanating from the mansion. Dominic reacted to the racial crack from Pansine. “Don’t take that shit too personal, okay Charley?”

Joco and his band of cutthroats had just entered and were met by a boiling Pansine. “It’s about time you fucking showed! This ain’t one of your pussy street deals. Look around,” he said, “it don’t get bigger than this.”

Tyrone, Joco’s hulking bodyguard, who looked like he could hunt wild bear with a switch, stepped forward. “Relax Frank,” he said. “You get too excited.”

“Frank, Frank!” Yelled Pansine, “Who the fuck you calling Frank? It’s Mr. Pansine to you punk. You think you hit the big time cause your watching his back?” nodding to Joco.

“You made your point man,” answered Joco. “Now let’s see your paper.”

“In time,” said Frank. “First the professor. Suit you?” asked Frank.

“Why not! He’s the best,” said Joco.

“You bet your sweet black ass he is,” answered Pansine.

All the men present adjourned to another room. Along the way Tyrone said to his boss, “I’m gonna stick that ginny prick.”

Back inside the police car Charley Sawyer was now grinning over to Dominic, "Don't take that shit too personal. OK Pap!"

The mansion incorporated many rooms but this particular one was quite unique. Most research laboratories throughout the world would pale in comparison. It was equipped in every possible way. Perhaps under different circumstances one might discover a cure for some lethal life-threatening disease or simply to prolong a young person's future. However, on this night its mission was to deal only in the selfish prospect of great financial profit.

A very sophisticated man looking all the world like a college professor of chemistry, which was exactly what he was, stepped forward. "Gentleman," he said, "shall we begin?"

Joco motioned to another one of his no-neck assistants nearby who promptly dropped a sample bag on the table. Everyone present had their own private thoughts and agendas while they all waited in quiet desperation for this solitary man to determine their monetary futures.

Joco's mind began rewinding way back to his humble beginnings. Every since he could remember he had been at war in one form or another. Joco, just plain Joco, as he was and is fear fully known.

He was the undisputed and unremorseful leader of the most vicious and feared gangs ever assembled in the Bronx, Los Assinos, English translation "The Killers" or "Assassins." They occupied every waking hour seeking out and eliminating rival gangs, anything or anybody that would stand in their way.

He was a slim, muscular, skin-headed, tattooed, 33-year-old, who treated killing as some sort of perverse sport. Like they, his victims, were all human game. He proudly composed rap lyrics about the pleasures he had felt taking human life.

His birth name was Joseph Devon Martinez. Abandoned by his nomad, asshole, Puerto Rican father early on and left to be raised by his poor, sickly African-American mother who tried her best but the call of the wild streets was too strong and attractive. Killing his way up the ladder to power and respect. He had taunted law enforcement when and wherever and had led sophisticated ambushes that had even ensnared members of the police in a barrage of gunfire. While locked up, on occasion, he had incited jail riots and assaulted guards. Responding to one such attack in which an officer survived, he was heard boasting, "Next time I'll have to stab him."

Whenever the authorities had arrested him and tried to prosecute, witnesses had either disappeared or when confronting this butcher in a court of law, backed away from statements against him they had given detectives. "Free once again. Who says crime doesn't pay?" He would rap out loud on the courthouse steps while thumbing his nose at society and every decent thing it stood for.

Ever since Chris and Jerry lost their precious, young lives that horrific night three years ago in Queens, Dominic has been plagued with a single nightmare of crushing guilt, the genuine reality that the bomb was most certainly meant for him alone. He was left with only two incentives in life. One was to continue raising up his granddaughter, Maria. The other was that he personally see to it that the monster known as Joco pay dearly. His vendetta was so powerful it had even motivated his temporarily pulling up roots to follow his prey some 3,500 miles west to sunny Southern California.

"Excellent!" said the professor, finishing his laborious task inside the house. "Best I've seen right out of the kitchen. One hundred percent pure cocaine. Should crack up nicely." Frank Pansine sent Johnny Brandoli for the money bag. Joco's eyes closely followed the young man while he ran his errand.

"Tell Murphy not to move until Johnny gives us the done deal sign, Dominic said to Charley.

"I hate to admit it Pap, but you were right about that rookie in their kids got two sets of balls," Charley answered Dominic.

"Remember it is absolutely critical the money change hands. We need the intent to sell angle. One last thing, my favorite partner, we'll catch them coming out. Pass it on. Hopefully they'll resist arrest and if we are real lucky after tonight six or eight of that scum bag Joco's associates will be carrying him by the handles."

Meanwhile everything and everybody seemed satisfied. Supply and demand was met.

Suddenly, and without warning, Joco pulled out a high caliber automatic shoulder pistol and fired only once, striking Johnny in the head and killing him instantly. The room came to a stop. "What the fuck's the matter with you?" yelled Pansine.

Joco reached down to the lifeless and bleeding boy, tore back his shirt and exposed a hidden wire for all to see. "I thought I smelled pizza! Fuck you Pappy," he said grinning into the miniature microphone.

"Shit!" screamed Dominic. "They hit the kid. Let's roll. Seal off all exits immediately."

An army of blue closed in on the mansion from every direction, all eager to kill or capture the sons of bitches responsible for killing a cop, brave, young Johnny Brandoli. Pansine, like all organized crime career hoods, had left open an escape route known only to himself. It was a secret wine cellar that was underground, left over from the early days of prohibition. Frank Pansine's only exit plan if needed was to make it out with at least his money. Half of the deal – and with luck the drugs to boot. He never intended for Joco and his crowd to leave the house alive. Joco's street instincts for survival under fire were to serve him well. He figured the double cross was in from the start. He too had planned on shooting his way out if needed. His boys were all armed with automatics, 16 shots per, and their loads packed with armor piercing and able to take down anything in sight.

Dominic was cautiously working his way around to the back of the house. Most of the heavy fire exchange took place inside and out front. He was met with a surprisingly amount of mild resistance, certainly nothing he couldn't handle. Shooting at paper targets was one thing, but killing another human being up close without hesitation was quite different. Dominic possessed this quality. Coupled with great hand-eye dexterity, you had the perfect killing machine. He and his six-shot revolver were still serving each other well. After taking out 2 shooters, both with head shots, Dominic finally had a chance to realize once and for all an end to his nightmare. Joco Martinez momentarily was directly within his line of fire. Dominic shot but his clear round was blocked by the massive bodyguard, Tyrone, who caught the slug in his right shoulder and allowed his boss to disappear into a cave-like darkness.

Charley Sawyer already well into this same tunnel was chasing Frank Pansine when Joco fired, hitting the officer in his lower back. This enabled both big shots to slip past all the blood and guts. Both men were away scot-free. As the smoke cleared Dominic ran up to his downed friend, slowing to a walk, expecting the worst. He leaned down to check for vitals.

This once quiet, well-protected neighborhood had exploded with gunfire resulting in several casualties.

"Damn!" reacted Charley. "Your hands are a hell of a lot colder than you obviously think I am."

"How bad?" asked Dominic.

"I don't feel a thing," said Charley. "What happened to our candy man?" he asked.

"Clean ass getaway," said Dominic. And it gets better, the money and the powder all gone. Unfucking real, we really pissed this away kid."

"Call my wife, will you Pap?"

"Roger that," said Dominic, putting his hand on his wounded buddy's shoulder just like he'd done countless times before with fallen comrades in Nam nearly forty years ago.

CHAPTER 3

Approximately 5 miles just west of the 405 freeway lied still another stronghold for the rich and famous, Brentwood, with its fair share of highly successful residents, mostly known for their superior creative talent and flawless beauty. Perhaps the one single group of the best-looking human beings ever assembled in one spot on God's earth, complete with an army of licensed nip-and-tuck neighbors hired occasionally to keep them in tune.

Alongside that slice of A-list picture royalty resided a few industrial men of entrenched wealth, old money dating back to the early California settlers.

Robert Powers most certainly qualified. His penniless great-grandfather won an oil lease from some obscure wildcatter in a poker game. That first well came in shortly before Henry Ford, Sr. started seriously manufacturing assembly line automobiles. The lease was smack in the middle of one of the largest and bottomless oil finds ever, Kettlemen Hills. That stroke of initial good luck was parlayed over and over again throughout the years.

By no means had this billionaire ever been satisfied with his status quo. Robert Powers had continually and with persistence led a most productive life in his 50-odd years. Like his father before him, he had reached out and worked alongside most of the world's great men and women, all doing their absolute best to constantly improve the human condition.

It was Friday morning around nine. The sun was well along on its daily rise. Perfect weather for a round or two of single tennis. The court had been completely dry for about an hour following last evening's unexpected rainfall. Even the birds were out and already hitting their best high notes. Lisa Powers had just served an ace against her philanthropic uncle, Robert Powers.

"Had enough?" she asked.

"Try as I might, I can't beat you, honey," answered Uncle Bob.

"I know," she said. "I'm on a roll."

Bob Powers walked over to his cabana in order to fix a couple of drinks.

"Too early for me, dear," she said.

"You coming Saturday, Lisa?" he asked.

"I hope you're not going to stick me with all those bureaucratical bores. I'll be there," Lisa said. "And alone if that helps you answer your next question."

"You can tell me to shut up, Lisa," he went on, "but I am going to get this said."

"You always do," she countered.

"When in the hell," he asked, "are you going to stop wasting your afternoons beating an old fart at tennis and get on with it?"

"It?" she asked.

"You know, it!" he said.

"Oh, that it. Well in the first place," she said, "I happen to have a fondness for beating old farts, especially when I adore their company, and in the second place my love life, such as it is, belongs to me. OK, Pal?" she asked.

"Could it be you are spending way too much of your time trying to change our planet?" he asked. "I've spent a lifetime dealing with those same issues, then one morning you wake up middle-aged and very alone."

"Now who's the bore?" she answered.

"Honey," he said, "when I got you that job at WKLT, I thought you would use this family's valuable connections to secure a safe and lucrative future. Instead I find you regularly up to your pretty young ass in lost causes. As far as I'm concerned this part of the world has gone to hell and it can stay there."

"So much for optimism," said Lisa.

Bob Powers picked up the morning paper from a nearby table and read the front page headline. "Case in point," he said, "drug czar beats the odds! You see, now they have got their poison in our own backyard."

Lisa studied the article with a trained eye. "I've got an idea," she said.

"I don't like it already," he said. "You always get that look when you are about to do something crazy."

"Daring maybe, crazy no. thanks for the game and your concern," said Lisa. "I love you Mr. Powers."

Lisa Powers and Maria Pisa both shared one common denominator, both were left fatherless at a very vulnerable age. Lisa was born 28 years ago to a privileged clan, one of extreme wealth and power, raised primarily by her classy and beautiful mother after her father's promising political career was cut short with a heart seizure at 38. Ever since that precious man introduced his little girl to the wonderful world of books, she had known that one day her life's work would take on some form of writing. Her real-life heroes growing up could not be found between the bindings of any fictional story. They were all alive and well broadcasting nightly out to millions of people throughout a troubled and ruthless world. Men like Kronkite, Brokaw, and the ever handsome Peter Jennings.

Her father's only surviving sibling was her uncle, Robert Powers, who had constantly over the years provided the male influence, even after her mother's untimely passing due to a stroke at 46. Those next few trying years for this now stunning beauty, inside and out, had brought the bond she enjoyed with her influential uncle only that more committed.

Dominic's walkup apartment was in a quiet section of Burbank, California. It was a comfortable neighborhood, as comfortable as it got on an honest cop's salary. Dominic's 9-year-old granddaughter, Maria, had just entered her grandpa's extremely dark bedroom which by now reeked of excessive cigarette smoke and Top Shelf scotch. She opened the windows, along with his blinds, to let the sunlight in and the bad air out. She discovered an ashtray filled to its brim from under a pillow. "Shit!" she yelled.

Dominic was coming around. "You better watch your mouth, young lady," he said. Then he mumbled something in Italian.

"I'm trying to make your bed, Papa," she answered.

"Well, you might have better luck if I weren't in it!" he said.

"Looks like you really blew it last night, huh?" she asked, while continuing to tidy things up.

Dominic was desperately trying to compose himself. "What's that supposed to mean?" he asked.

"Because whenever you screw up, you get fried," she answered.

"Why aren't you in school?" he asked.

"I wanted to see if you were all right. Jamie's mom is taking us. I told her you were sick, Papa."

"Close!" he said. "Have yourself a great day, baby. You need any money?" he asked.

"I already took it," Maria said.

He once again mumbled something else in Italian.

"Watch your mouth, Papa. I speak it too, you know."

"Sorry, baby. Haven't you forgotten something?" he asked.

Maria leaned back into the doorway and kissed Dominic on the cheek.

Maria Pisa was a beautiful mixture physically between her father, Jerry's, dark, thick hair and her grandmother Sophia's piercing green eyes and olive skin. Add her late mother, Chris', wonderful Irish wit and you had quite a package.

This very young girl had been subjected to more than any human being should have to endure in any lifetime. She had survived through it all with amazing poise and had shown incredible resiliency; qualities rarely found in one so brand new.

Dominic gradually made his way about with a minimum of effort. One mustn't move too quickly when hung over. He was trying to reach his cellphone. Thank God for speed dial, he thought. After what seemed like an eternity someone finally picked up.

"Garcia here."

"Johnny is that you?" asked Dominic. "Is Captain Stillwell around?"

"He just stepped out to meet with some VIP," Garcia said. "He told all of us that when you called to apologize for last night's party. He'd see you promptly at 2 p.m. sharp, his office. Oh, and Pappy," said Garcia, "if you've got a hat I suggest you humbly carry it! HA!" laughed Garcia.

"Hey, Johnny," said Dominic, "you know what you can do with that hat, and what I heard about that time you worked deep cover on a case down in county, it just might fit!"

"Fuck you, Pisa," said Johnny.

Bad days with their evil deadlines just seem to come at you a hell of a lot quicker than the positive ones. Before what seemed to Dominic like a blink of an eye, he was surrounded in a room with huge collective negatives. Hollywood Precinct, which was Pisa's home court, usually represented, to him, happier times. No one relished the thought of failure but to have it rubbed in your face publicly took a strong-willed commitment.

"Hi, Pappy," said police woman Donna Garrett. "I understand the mayor is looking for a few good men to watch his house Friday night. One of those fundraisers, what with all the diamonds and furs floating around he may be in need of a little expert assistance," she laughed.

"Sure, sweetheart," replied Dominic, "but I'll only go on one condition, you go along as backup, get really wasted and sit on my face!"

"Bastard!" yelled Donna. "I'll have you up on charges."

"Sexual harassment?" he questioned. "At my age how you gonna make it stick?" he asked. "Besides most of the guys here in this happy gathering have seen those revealing photos you proudly display on your personal web site. Oh! And what an unusual spot for a tattoo."

Captain Stillwell had seen his still top officer through the glass perimeter surrounding his office and motioned him to come ahead.

"Dominic," he said, "we were just discussing you."

Dominic's curious eyes worked the room as he spotted Lisa Powers for the first time. "Why should you be any different, Captain?" said Dominic.

"Lisa Powers meet Lieutenant Dominic Pisa," said Stillwell.

Lisa extended her rather surprisingly firm hand. "Pleasure, Mr. Pizza. I've heard a lot of good things about you."

"That's Pisa, as in leaning tower of, not as in hold the anchovies," he replied.

"We were just reading your review in today's Times," she said sarcastically.

"Hum," said Dominic, "did they get my name right?"

"Aren't you being a bit cavalier, Lieutenant?" she asked. "After all you did shoot up half the city last evening."

"And the bad guys shot up the other half," he answered. "Say, what the hell is this boss?" he asked.

"Relax, Dominic," said Stillwell, "Miss Powers represents WKLT-TV. I'll let her fill you in."

"Lieutenant," she said, "when I saw those headlines I decided that the correct way to approach our problem."

"Our problem?" Dominic interrupted.

"This city's serious problem of drugs and organized crime," said Lisa. "I think it's about time my viewers found out first hand just what's being done to fight this cancer."

"First hand!" he replied.

"Yes," said Lisa, "I have suggested and George here, referring to Stillwell, agrees that it would be a good idea if I rode with you and your men so I could capture the full impact of what's really going on out there."

"Well, if George here," he grumbled, "doesn't mind, I do! And about the only thing, young lady, you are going to capture in that sewer out there is a high-caliber slug.

"See here, Pisa!" Lisa said, "I'm trying to give you and your department a little well needed public relations. Perhaps you should reevaluate your position."

Dominic about to blow, "You want to know my position, lady?" he said, "I have got one dead brave young officer and a partner in the hospital with a bullet that has become part of his spine. My position is to do my level best to see that the son of a bitch that pulled the trigger gets his share of the needle."

Captain Stillwell could see the young reporter was not going to get her way bumping heads with this aging keeper of the keys. "Miss Powers, will you excuse us?" he asked. "I'm sure the lieutenant and I will come to some understanding."

Lisa graciously left in minor defeat. Stillwell began his verbal assault. Anger became rage, excelling to near insanity which receded as Dominic was ushered out.

"Well, if you put it that way, boss, it makes a lot more sense," said Dominic."

"I thought you would see the wisdom, Pappy. We'll start this thing Monday evening sharp."

Seated around a massive conference table located high above ground level, occupying one of many luxurious office buildings that pepper Century City were a select few consisting largely of self-centered men of longstanding within the community.

"That's all well and good, gentlemen," stated a very defensive Joco Martinez. "But you all don't seem to realize the pressure I'm under."

"Sir, may I point out," said one of the eight distinguished men around the table, "that you and your people are more than compensated for your efforts."

"Just the tip of the iceberg, man," said Joco.

"Bottom line," said a second man, "is that our last six month's profits have receded drastically. Why?"

"I can answer that in two words," Joco answered, "Dominic Pisa."

"I beg your pardon," said a third man, "did I hear you correctly? Do we know him?" he asked, looking about the huge room for an answer.

Still another man pulled out a file and began to read. "Lieutenant Dominic Pisa, formerly of New York P.D., transferred for no apparent reason to the Los Angeles force approximately two years ago. A widower, lost his wife of 35 years four years ago to cancer. He has a 9-year-old granddaughter who lives with him following his son's, also an officer, and his daughter-in-law's untimely deaths due to a car bombing three and a half years ago. He is one of the most decorated officers in the department including a gold shield, knows the streets like an alley cat and has never been bought. Very impressive," said the chairman seated where he belongs at the head of this tidy group.

"Still and all only one man. Why not have our Mr. Joco here make this go away?" he asked.

"It won't be easy," answered Joco. "This wop cop has been a constant thorn in my ass for years."

"That is none of our affair," answered the chairman, "See to it!" he ordered.

High-end automobiles were arriving for Robert Powers Saturday night gala. His elaborate and richly decorated home was filling to capacity with most of Southern California's leading movers and shakers. Lisa Powers had just arrived and was looking about the beautiful rooms for a familiar face. She spotted her uncle sharing a cocktail with Judge Manville Parks, certainly one of LA's top legal giants, and his wife.

Bob Powers signaled his niece to join them. "Lisa, honey," he said, "glad you could make it. Judge Parks, you remember my niece?" he asked.

"Of course, Bob, how could I forget my favorite news hound? How is it going over at WKLT?" he asked. "Your boss, Bill Curtis, still owes me fifty bucks on last week's Laker game."

"I'm sure he's good for it, sir," she answered.

"You know my wife, Lucille?" asked the judge.

"Of course. How have you been Mrs. Parks?"

"Fine Lisa," she answered.

"You know, judge, I'm putting together something downtown that just may interest you," said Lisa.

"Really," he replied, "and what might that be?"

"There is a first-rate story out there dealing with drugs and gang violence," she said, "and I intend to get it."

"Well, young lady, I wish you a lot of luck. How may I ask do you intend on going about it?"

"I have made arrangements to ride along with one of our finest police lieutenants," she answered.

"Who? Maybe I know him," he questioned.

"Dominic Pisa," replied Lisa.

The mood quickly changed to the negative. "Bob," said Judge Parks, "nice party. Wish we could stay, got a full schedule. Call me first of the week, we'll take lunch at the Pacific Dining Car, my treat. Lisa always a pleasure."

Both Powers bid farewell. "What was that all about," she asked.

"They probably just had to go. Relax," said Bob. "Come on, sweetheart."

"You saw that look on his face when I mentioned that policeman's name. You would of thought he'd just been recalled."

"Lisa, I didn't think that you could top your past record for irresponsibility," he said, "but going out into the streets it worries the hell out of me!"

"I'll be fine, dear," said Lisa. "Mr. Pisa may be rough and hard edged but he is effective."

"Well, he better be, you're all I have," said Bob Powers.

"Now be a saint and please fetch me a drink," asked Lisa.

Dominic was spending his Saturday night renewing his love affair with twelve-year-old scotch straight up and listening to whatever Sinatra recorded in his prime Fifties era, mellowing through a terrific sound system at his favorite watering hole called "Jake's for Drinks." Jake's was a definite throwback to the bars you might find in an old black and white early Mitchum film. It was a place where people from all walks of life gathered to share a common passion for fine food and great drink. A single was a double and a double was a triple shot. These were serious, world-class drinkers dating back to Hollywood's Golden Era. Between 1936 and 1956 when it was known then as "The Lobby" where you could find on any given evening the likes of Errol Flynn or John Barrymore, or even the King himself, Clark Gable, blowing off a little well needed steam. It was called The Lobby originally because its globetrotting clientele would bring back from wherever they had been worldwide hotel keys, which then were proudly displayed over the back bar. Its ceiling was an unusual color of reddish-brown. Legend had it the rare stain was brought on by excessive tobacco smoke.

Jake bought the place back in 1990 when it fell on hard times following the original owner's death at 92. Jake had done his level best to keep the place in its original décor.

Jake Bartlett looked like someone from 40 or 50 years ago, proudly wearing the abuse he had self-inflicted over decades of ingesting all sorts of substances, both legal and otherwise. He was a pleasant man most of the time and he enjoyed people, the highly successful ones, no matter what their field.

Homicide detective and one of Dominic's favorite drinking buddies, Chet Higgins, had just arrived. "How many am I behind, Pap?" he asked.

Dominic held up three fingers. "What kept you?"

Chet motioned to Jake behind the bar for another round. "Late-breaking event," answered Chet. "They found this young dead hooker over off of Sunset in a ditch."

"Runaway?" asked Dominic.

"Don't know yet, no ID."

"Did she overdose?" asked Dominic.

"Nope, definitely foul play, broken neck."

"Well at least it's clean," said Dominic.

"Clean my ass. She was blood from one orifice to the other," said Chet, tossing down a drink. "Well, I'm back on the run, Pap, got a tip from one of my ace snitches. Enjoy yourself then call a cab. OK buddy?"

Jake walked over to pick up Chet's empty glass. "How goes the percentage, Lieutenant?" he asked.

"I'll let you know around closing," said Dominic.

"I'm real sorry about Johnny and your partner," said Jake.

"That's why we sign on, comes with the badge," Dominic said. "You know, Jake, you're not such a bad guy. I even get to smoke in here and on top of that you even serve honest liquor."

"You ready for a little more honesty, Lieutenant?" asked Jake.

“Is there any left?” said Dominic.

“Stop trying to carry the world around on your back. Fuck em!” said Jake. “If people want to kill themselves with booze, pot, cocaine, crack, pills or any other goddamn mind-altering shit, let them! You won’t even make a dent.”

“Well another fucking optimist is heard from,” said Dominic.

A large, tough-looking man in his late forties had been watching this debate from a nearby table. He had taken offense at Dominic’s reply. He approached the bar heading straight towards Dominic. “Jake was right!” said the stranger. “If people want to party down and enjoy themselves, it’s none of your goddamn business. What are you, some kind of Dirty Harry or just a misguided dick head with a big brother complex?” he yelled.

Dominic’s anger began to swell. He was not having even a little bit more of this hulk. He grabbed an empty long neck beer bottle from the bar just as the man lunged, and with split timing smashed the ugly man’s face, sending him ass over backwards through a set of tables. Dominic displayed his badge while looking down on his much younger prey. “That’s Mr. Dick Head to you, and it does happen to be my business. Sorry, Jake,” said Dominic, “about this but a man my age can’t afford to be assaulted.”

“Yeah,” said Jake grinning, “I can see that.”

Joco was holding court with a few associates and the best looking women money could buy. Everyone was gathered around his penthouse apartment for a business meet. “Boys,” said Joco, “we’re still gonna roll on Whitey but with a twist. From time to time I’ll need some of your firepower. We'll start making key hits all over town. stir up the shit big time. Look like drive-bys but we all know better. Got it?" he asked.

"Yes, sir, I heard that," said one boy.

"Now listen carefully," said Joco, "we're gonna start all this with the king pig himself. Guy named Dominic Pisa."

"Say, I know him," said a second boy, Darren Dillard, looking all the world like a younger version of his idol, Joco. "Old guy! Right? Come down on one of my homies hard man," said Darren. "Be my pleasure. What's our end?" he asked.

"Smart kid," Joco said. "I'll see you get something real big next time out. Should level a fucking city block."

"When and where?" asked Darren.

"He won't be much to find," said Joco, "likely he be up your young black ass most nights. So down and dirty on this one boys, down and dirty."

Mondays were difficult enough without having to face four more nights of the same unknown. It used to be years back when a cop strapped on his gun and badge most evenings would be occupied with simply just driving around neighborhoods, having to present a show of force. No one then but a crazy hooligan, as they were known, would dare physically challenge an officer's authority. Today was a new deal, baby. There seemed to be armies out there who would go a mile out of their way just to get a clear shot at a black and white. It was justice in the streets.

Maria had just walked in on her grandfather as she had countless times over the past few years. "You should trade in that old Saturday night special, Papa," she said.

"Get yourself a nine millimeter Glock. It's got two to one fire power."

"Really," said Dominic, "and thank you Bruce Willis. I told the sitter, Mrs. Cooper, that I want your homework done and your cute butt in bed by nine."

"Ah, Papa. There is a show on I want to see," she replied.

"I can just imagine. Some more of that reality crap," Dominic said. "Anyway someone in this family has got to get a decent education."

"Why?" asked Maria. "I can just grow up and be a cop like you."

"Or maybe a standup comic," he said. "Bedtime is still nine sharp."

Maria looked up to the sky as if it were heaven. "Grownups," she cried, "why do they always have to be in charge?"

CHAPTER 4

Dominic's home court, Hollywood Division, was probably the most active of them all during the day. This glamourous and historic section of L.A. was buzzing with the sights and sounds of tourists.

Moms and pops from anywhere USA had all gathered with their mixed batch of heirs for the excitement originating daily from that now famous intersection of Hollywood and Highland. Any day was a thrilling one for the out of towners. However, the evenings took on a whole different new meaning. What came out with the stars at night was something else again.

If they didn't have it there in Tinsel Town, they simply didn't make it. Two miles south of Hollywood Blvd. lied another famous street, Santa Monica Blvd., complete with all of its she-men prancing proudly around in drag looking to make their daily bread. Back north you had one of the most celebrated streets in the world; they even dedicated a movie to it, Sunset Blvd. Once the home of "The Garden of Allah", a beautiful Spanish court known for its famous swimming pool surrounded by a dozen or so private and sinful bungalows just off the pool. To the right was a quaint little bar, another popular spot for serious drinking, dancing or just plain raising all sorts of hell. Men and women of letters would collect there on a regular basis to practice their writer's disease, alcohol, no less than Dorothy Parker, F. Scott Fitzgerald, Robert Benchly, Will Fowler, and so on and so on. This all went away in the early seventies when a Bank and Trust bought the buildings plus 2 acres and leveled it. Now in its beautiful past resided still another goddamn strip mall complete with, you guessed it, McDonald's, sharing center stage to a bevy of equally appalling fast food whatevers, directly across the street on Highland and Sunset, once the spot that housed Swab's Drugstore, now barely remembered for its famous daily patrons and their timely gossip.

All those wonderful landmarks and safe havens for the rich and famous were all gone, vanished, and in their places, now lied in the quiet nightly shadows, crimes of all shapes and sizes just waiting patiently for opportunity. The criminal mind experts all agree does exist and will begin to once again exercise its routine prerogative.

Dominic Pisa was walking out the back of his precinct with a few fellow officers, joking with each other.

Lisa Powers was seated shotgun and waiting impatiently. Dominic reached for his door handle which was locked. "Really lady," said Dominic. "What in the hell do you think is going to happen to you here sitting in an armed police car in a precinct parking lot surrounded by blue coats and badges? The bad guys are all out there," pointing to the streets.

"Sorry," she said, unlocking his door. "Force of habit."

"You keep locking doors and you just might miss a whole lot of life this fucking world holds for us all."

"Can we just forego the four letter lecture lieutenant?" said Lisa.

Dominic started the car. "Just my New York alphabet creeping out, fucking A, fucking B, fucking C. Ha!" He laughed, pushing in a fresh CD while firing up an unfiltered Camel cigarette, just as he had done ever since he was a 17 year old in boot camp at Paris Island. He took a deep, rewarding first drag like it was his last, savored the taste then exhaled with a cloud of smoke. The music sounded off with a rousing jazz number interpreted by the late and great Benny Goodman and his Sextet. He was having himself one hell of a time.

Lisa could not believe her eyes, let alone her ears. "Lieutenant Pisa would you mind putting out that awful thing?" She asked, waving the smoke away. "And while you're at it, lower the noise level about three octaves."

He immediately pulled the car over to a complete stop. "Let us lay down a few hard rules here," He said. "My car, my radio and my space in which I do whatever and whenever the spirit moves me."

"Smoking is a filthy, barbaric habit. Didn't you read the Surgeon General's warnings on its hazards?" She asked.

"If it wasn't in the sports page I missed it," answered Dominic. "As far as the noise level is concerned, that is probably the greatest clarinet player the world will ever know. Benny Goodman. Now I don't want to be rude, but what we have here is a bad situation. So you have got to make the best of it."

"In the first place," she replied, "you most certainly do want to be rude. It happens to be your nature and you love it. And in the second place I suspect that under that rough exterior of yours beats the heart of a certified bully."

"I'll take that as a compliment," he countered, "and as for these," exhaling once again, "I wouldn't trust anyone without at least two filthy habits."

CHAPTER 5

In sharp contrast to the depressed area which was Dominic's beat, we traveled across town to a place society tells us represents success, complete with all of its trappings. The overgrown house with its fleet of shining foreign cars to decorate her expansive circular driveway and inside her owners surrounded themselves with an unusual amount of diamonds, furs and the like, endowed to them by one Manville P. Parks and his several digit income. He had sired two heirs by his solid wife of thirty-seven years, one grown son, a prominent Boston attorney, the other a 16-year-old daughter spoiled beyond belief.

Amanda Parks, in her relatively short life had managed a multitude of sins. Lately her energies were preoccupied with the busy end of a crack pipe.

Young Amanda was about to leave her well-secured and protected mansion for another one of her misadventures. Her mother reluctantly headed her off.

"Where do you think you're going, Mandy?" She asked.

"Jenny's," answered Amanda.

"Jenny who? Do we know her?"

"Jenny Baxter. Remember mother? They moved here about a month ago."

"It's a bit late and a school night, dear."

"Mother, really!" Snapped Amanda, "Let's not be a bore."

"You are only sixteen," said her mother.

"I'm just going down the block for Christ sake," said Amanda.

"That's no way to speak to your mother, Mandy," said Judge Manville Parks, coming down the rich spiral staircase.

"When are you and mother both going to wake up to the fact I'm a grown woman?" Amanda asked. "I have asked you both repeatedly to please call me by my given name, Amanda."

"That's quite enough! Go to your room," he yelled. "We will discuss this in the morning."

"Always tomorrow," Amanda said, "and always your way."

"This is my house and my roof and while you're under it you'll obey me, young lady! Now go to your room and stay there!" He screamed up the stairs.

CHAPTER 6

Dominic and Lisa began their evening on a slow note, routinely moving about the dark and seedy side of town under Dominic's ever suspicious eye. Suddenly he spotted a familiar face. The subject, realizing the consequences, pushed his way past a crowded street and into a nearby bar. Dominic slammed on his brakes, nearly driving Lisa out of her expensive high heels, and gave chase. He approached the club's entrance only to be stopped by the bouncer, an extremely burly man, built like a linebacker.

"Good evening, young man," said Dominic, flashing his ID. "I'm sorry to bother you but that scum bag that just ran in here, you see where he went?"

The bouncer grinned, "You got to be kidding, man. That could be half the joint!"

Dominic pressed past the action and out into the dimly lit back alley. A firm believer that a strong defense is an overpowering offense, he armed himself with an old and dependable dear friend, his snub-nose thirty-eight revolver. He cautiously made his way down the damp and highly dangerous passageway with all of its foul odors and unknowns, back out into the main thoroughfare.

Meanwhile the local street types had began milling about Dominic's police car, observing its well-scrubbed passenger as a lioness would fresh meat. With a surge of fear Lisa quickly slapped at the power locks. The crowd began to recede as Dominic cut his way, empty-handed, back through to his once again secured car door.

"I know, don't say it," said Lisa, "but this is hardly a precinct and this tidy group is the last thing from blue coats."

Dominic grinned as he reached in for his radio, "This is Pisa one-700 requesting a make on a Lester Mercer, alias Lester Brooks. I'll hold." He paused for a moment. "You got a current address? Shit! Well, fax what you do have off to New York City, Manhattan South, see what they come up with." Dominic was eagerly waiting for a reply. "What's that I got a call from who? Well, where the hell is she? Got it, thanks baby. If this tip pans out it's dinner on me. Anything more you'll have to bring help."

In what seemed to be one single movement he placed his speaker back onto its hook, started the car and peeled off with enough accelerated speed to wear off 1,000 miles of tread to his rear tires.

"I thought the chase came later," joked Lisa.

"A free-base junkie has just given birth over at County General," said Dominic.

"Lieutenant, babies are born every day."

"Not Joco's," he replied.

"What's a Joco?"

He ignored the question. The bright city lights breezed by as Dominic continued accelerating towards the hospital. His only thoughts and hopes were that this young mother might shed some new light on her Latin stallion's whereabouts, anything that could brighten up this old man's day. They pulled up to the ER and were immediately met by a doctor shaking his head.

While Dominic was busy elsewhere Lisa noticed a newborn nearby in an incubator jumping about to the point of seizure. Showing her press credentials she moved towards the attending nurse. “What’s wrong with the baby?” she asked.

“He was born an addict!” answered the nurse.

“What are his chances?”

“On crack? Low for survival and even less for a normal life,” answered the nurse.

“Take a good look, Miss Powers,” said Dominic, “this is where it starts,” looking to the baby, “and that’s where it all ends,” pointing to the dead and burned out mother. “This is no longer a case where a select few bucks up button down type kids are getting high, it’s fucking war and every mother and father had better get off their naïve asses and join the fight. Statistics show that eight out of ten children have tried drugs in one form or another and rock or crack cocaine accounts for roughly 90 percent of street seizures.”

“That’s terrible,” said the nurse.

“So is farting, but we all do it,” said Dominic walking away.

“Charming, isn’t he?” said Lisa to the nurse.

CHAPTER 7

A deserted neighborhood street just like any other you might find at nine o'clock at night across America. But this was South Central Los Angeles and just a little more so. The street was empty except for an elderly black couple walking their terrier. The old man was putting his arm around the old woman, who seemed to be enjoying the moment, as if it had happened before.

"Honey," she said, "You still know how to make a girl feel to home.

"Baby," he said, "There wouldn't be a home if it weren't for you. Always an incurable romantic and I wouldn't have it any other way."

She gleamed.

The small dog was going about sniffing for whatever the hell all dogs sniff for. A low-riding car turned the corner from the north, pulled to a stop and ejected two black teenage boys.

"Thanks for the ride, man. Later on Homes," said one boy.

"Be careful, Jackie," said the driver. "The streets are hot! Real hot."

"We can take care of our own shit, man!" said the second boy. "They wouldn't fuck with us round here, no way."

A second low-rider car turned right and made its way south towards the first car. Its radio was heard in the distance, the bass became almost deafening as it approached closer and louder to a cruise, facing almost exactly opposite the first car. Its windows, tinted beyond recognition, slowly powered down exposing a heavy arsenal. The sights and sounds of semiautomatic fire began raking the area and before the target car could retaliate, it was over. This once quiet street was now awash with the blood of its young victims. The assault vehicle disappeared down the block screaming past its frightened audience.

The old woman was on her knees in shock, shielding her ears from the deafening cries of death.

Death in a neighborhood she had shared with her loving husband, who was at her side, and had been for more than forty years. "Baby! It's all right. You're not hit. I'm not hit. It's gonna be all right."

She looked up, wiping away her tears while looking around. "There are dead babies here. This can never be right. My God, what has happened to us? What have we done to our children for them to make war on each other? Where is God," She asked, "to let this happen?"

Amanda Parks' bedroom was something to behold with its high-beamed ceilings and rich décor. Her giant Hollywood king-sized pillow top mattress covered with endless soft and fluffy designer down sheets and duvets. Around the room it was furnished with all the latest electronic necessities a young girl needed to survive, from a 42-inch flat-screen, high-definition television set to the latest Apple laptop, to her brand new I-phone on which she was very busy trying to convince her girlfriend down the block to join her for an evening of unbelievable excitement.

“Don’t be such a joke, Jenny,” she said. “You’ll love this guy, he’s gorgeous! Now meet me down at my front gate in fifteen and don’t be late!”

CHAPTER 8

Dominic and Lisa had entered into what appeared to be organized confusion. Very noisy, telephones constantly ringing, people coming and going, just about what you would expect in a 24-7 rehabilitation clinic. One gang member was being interviewed by his current parole officer. "Come on, Lady! I'm tellin you the man is full of shit! Understand? Ain't no way I violated. He's out to fuck me over."

"Now why would the officer deliberately lie?" asked the parole officer.

"Hell. You blind? I'm black, that's all the reason that cracker needs!"

"Well, James, aren't we being just a bit paranoid? And another thing, watch your mouth!"

"Lady, I been on my own for most of my young years. Ain't had much time for books and school learnin. So keep it simple."

"Simply put, son," she said, "you tested positive and I don't need an officer's word for that. I'm sorry but my report will have to read negative."

"Please, they'll send me back to juvie."

Lisa reacted to witnessing this interplay. "That's so sad," she said.

"Sad! Give me a fucking break. That's no ordinary kid! He's a full on threat," said Dominic.

"Threat to who?" she asked.

"To me for one. I wouldn't turn my back on him for a New York minute."

"He's only a boy."

I'll tell you what he is," motioning for the parole officer's file and jacket, "May I?" asked Dominic putting on his 325 strength reading glasses, "Let's see here, hmm, James Slater, alias Jimmy Brooks, alias Albert Slater and so on and so on, 2004 arrested for grand theft. That same year booked again several times for forgery and stolen script. When he was fourteen he hit the big time. Says here he stuck his father with an ice pick while he was sleeping and he's been in and out of the system ever since. James, you better cancel Christmas, sport, you've been more naughty than nice!"

"Nice this!" said the boy, making an obscene gesture. "I got your sport hangin!" he yelled while they carted him off to finish serving whatever.

A mother was crying while her husband and daughter looked on. "I can't understand you, Pat!" the mother said while they all three sat at still another desk nearby. "We've always given you what we could. You must know your father here and I love you."

The father interrupted, "What the hell is with you, Pat?" he asked, "Putting your mother and me through all this crap and how can you do this to yourself? Putting that shit into your body?"

Young Patricia was just sitting there high, obviously on the nod.

"Mr. and Mrs. Parkins," said the counselor, "your girl, Pat, has been here before, so I'll only say this once. I'll send her home with you this time on the following conditions: One, she checks in and tests each and every day for a period of three weeks. And two, she is to attend school classes on a regular basis and is to maintain a B average. Is that understood?"

"Oh, yes, and thank you," said Mr. Parkins, "and may God bless you."

"I appreciate that sir," said the counselor. "However, I think Patricia here is in more need of inspired guidance. Good day."

"It's all so depressing," said Lisa. "That kid, James, what a hardcore. Who gets the blame for him?"

"Three generations of losers, that's his history. As far as his future goes, I'd say he's an odd-on favorite to blow it big time," said Dominic.

"What do you base that on?" she asked.

"He's an addict and a smoker with a $300-a-day crack monkey on his back and in order to support that he has to break the law. That means dealing, and as he gets bigger as a dealer, that's if he lives long enough, the deals get bigger. Then one day he fosters a few illegitimate kids of his own and the process starts all over again."

Dominic looked down at his watch which read nine thirty p.m. He whipped the car about to his left and headed off toward his place and parked exactly in front.

"What now?" asks Lisa.

"Relax," he answered. "I'll be right back."

He entered, leaving the front door ajar. He worked his way towards Maria's room which was dark except for the flickering light from the DVD "Seven". Dominic leaned down to kiss his granddaughter. Suddenly he pulled back the sheets to discover Maria fully dressed.

"Pappy!" she screamed.

"Maria!" he yelled back. "Is this how you mind?"

"But Pap, it's Brad Pitt and he's playing a police officer."

"Brad Pitt, arm pit, I don't care. Honey," he said, "I told you nine o'clock. Besides cops don't look like that. They look like me or worse."

"He's right!" said Lisa, who had been standing behind Dominic in the doorway. "And I agree, Brad Pitt is something to stay up for. Those eyes."

"Who's that? She's pretty," whispered Maria.

"Go to sleep, baby. I'll be home in a few hours."

"I'm sorry, Mr. Pisa. I must of dozed off," said the sitter, Mrs. Cooper.

"Well try and keep your eye on the ball. This kid is my life now, so don't let me down."

"Yes, sir! I won't," she answered.

Dominic turned off the set and began to join Lisa in the hall. "Night kid," he said. "You can finish watching Brad tomorrow."

Back at the car Lisa had a thought. "I get it!" she said, "hard core, soft center."

"All that in there is strictly off the record so lay off!" barked Dominic.

"My readers are mine!" she countered. "They just might want to know the kind of men they hire to protect and serve."

"That's a laugh," said Dominic. "The people don't give a damn unless it affects them personally."

"I don't buy that," she said.

"You've got me confused with someone who might give a shit!"

"You're beginning to wear thin, Pisa!" she said.

"You mean the magic is gone already?" said Dominic.

"You want me to give you a break? Well it goes both ways. After all, we're supposed to be partners," she said.

"Partners," he yelled, "not by any stretch. When some asshole shooter crawls out of the pavement and decides this is his big day for cops are you going to watch my back?" asked Dominic. "Lady, that's a partner. When you can do that we'll talk. Until then, get in." he said, pointing to the car.

Amanda Parks and her reluctant girlfriend, Jenny Baxter, were enjoying the excitement at a place called the Joy Box. It's a private night spot for the A-celebrity crowd, catering to young money, members only. Amanda spotted a handsome, young blonde boy as he approached the girls. "Hi Derek. What's up?" she asked.

"You know, baby, or you wouldn't be here. Who's your friend?" asked Derek.

"Jenny. She's cool," answered Amanda.

"Well she better be. The man doesn't like surprises."

"Well, when do we go?" she asked.

"How about now?" he said.

CHAPTER 9

Charley Sawyer was considered a veteran with 18 years on the job. He and Dominic hit it off right from the get go, even though Dominic was his senior by more than twenty years. Charley was Dominic's kind of cop, very good instincts with plenty of guts. He had kicked in more than his share of dangerous doors, first man in.

Dominic was peeking into his injured partner's hospital room. Charley spotted the old man out of the corner of his left eye. "What the hell you want?" asked Charley.

"How about your autograph?"

"How do you like this shit," said Charley, "I watch your ass and get mine blown off in the process. You owe me, pal, more than you know, buddy.

"How's the wound?" asked Dominic.

"Doesn't look like I'll be chasing any bad guys for a while, anyway," answered Charley.

"What about your wife?"

"I hope I don't have to chase her," said Charley.

"I meant how is she holding up?" Dominic asked.

"She's a cop's wife. What can I say." He answered.

Dominic was changing the subject. "Listen, the night of the shootout you said you thought you recognized one of the voices on that tape."

"I said one guy's name sounded familiar, that's all, Dom."

"That's all!" said Dominic. "Well it's a hell of a lot more than I got!"

"That thin, huh, Pap?"

"Think you could nail him if I brought the tape by?"

"It's worth a try, Pap.

"Well, we got to get back to the show," said Dominic.

"We?" asked Charley. "You cheaping around on me with a new backup already?"

"Not a chance, kid. Just some high level young female press jockey they stuck me with."

"Young?" asked Charley with a grin. "Well don't let that New York vocabulary of yours get away from you."

"Get some rest partner, I'll see you tomorrow, asshole."

Dominic quietly left the room, only to be met by Charley's wife, Irene, and their 13-year-old boy, Josh. "He looks good, Irene."

"Looks can be deceiving. It could have been worse, Pap," she said. "You could have got him killed but then he might as well be, he'll never walk again. Course he doesn't know it yet!"

"Take it easy, mom," said Charley's son, Josh.

"I'm worn out, Pap," she said. "Beaten down with worry. Seventeen years of worry. Now we're out of it. No more lying awake nights alone wondering if your husband is stretched out in some filthy hole with a bullet in his head. No more wondering. How much do we give? How much,

Pap? Your son and his wife both killed violently." Shaking her head, "I'm tired," she said. "Now I just want peace. I'm worn out." She disappeared into Charley's room.

"She's shook up, I give her that. But that's not Irene," he said. "She's always been a good cop's wife."

"You mean seen and not heard," said Lisa.

"You don't understand," said Dominic.

"You're right!" answered Lisa.

"What did you say?" asked Dominic, very puzzled when she agreed.

"You still don't get it, Mr. Pisa," she said. "That's why I'm here, I need your help. And I've got another flash for your, lieutenant; I'm really, truly on your side. I too would like to see you get the bastard, as you put it, that pulled the trigger."

CHAPTER 10

It goes without saying that not all the four-star rated hotels in the greater Los Angeles County area had employees who practiced the world's oldest occupation or, at the very least, subsidized that illegal behavior for their fair share of the cash. However, the ones that did stood to make on any busy convention-ridden weekend land office profits. When the demand exceeded the supply the ones that ponied up got secretly rich!

The dark décor of the Versailles Room, which was located in a quiet corner just off the lobby of the Landmark, a high rise hotel overlooking LAX was made to order. Wally Daniels, a ruggedly handsome, 50-year-old bartender had just gotten off his expensive I-phone. Casually he moved towards a pretty young redhead seated alone and drinking watered-down liquor. Leaning down to her, he whispered, "I got a hot one. He's in 540."

"You discuss price?" she asked.

"You bet your sweet young ass. And sugar, don't forget daddy over here."

"Sure Wally, see you in about an hour."

The pretty girl was just stepping of the elevator's fifth floor stop. She headed down the hall searching both sides for her designated number, counting to herself out loud while others passed by observing this strange behavior.

Finally she arrived at 540, or was it 450, she thought. A girl in her line of work couldn't afford to write things down. She shouldn't have had that last apple martini. Oh! What the hell. She took a run for the roses and knocked. The door to 540 opened exposing a darkened interior. The pretty girl was standing in the doorway, backlit by a hot hallway accentuating her spectacular figure.

"Hello, is anybody home?" she asked. There was complete silence. "Come on, I don't play games. Wally sent me, said you needed some company." Still total silence. You could hear a pin drop. Not even a breath was heard. She turned around as if to exit back to the elevator but was stopped by a strange voice.

"What's your name?" the voice asked the young girl who came to a halt with her back still facing the room. His voice was raspy almost to a fault. Certainly beyond the realm of sexy. "I said, what's your name?" he asked again. "You have one I presume."

"Yeah! I got a name," she said hesitantly. "But who cares? What's in a name? I didn't come here to talk!"

"What did you come up for? Tell me. I want to hear," he asked.

"You know, quit the bullshit. What are you, a cop?" she asked angrily.

"On the contrary, I hate cops," the voice said laughingly. "Won't you join me?"

She did an about face and made her way back into the room. "I don't know about this. Why are all the lights out?" she asked. "You got somebody else in here? If this is kinky it's gonna cost you guys. I don't do kink less I make double."

The raspy voice still deep into the room continued to bait the young whore. "Close the door behind you," he ordered, “then I’ll turn on the lights. I’m a very prominent man. I don’t want to be recognized. Does that sound fair to you?” he asked.

“Fuck it!” said the young girl. “Wally said you’re all right, let’s get busy.”

Amanda, Jenny and Derek had just arrived at Joco’s high-rise digs.

“Business must be good,” said Amanda, looking about the elaborate and private lobby.

“He does all right,” said Derek.

“He’s cute,” whispered Jenny to Amanda. “But I still don’t know about this. I got a bad feeling.”

“Jenny Baxter, don’t you dare embarrass me. Don’t be such a damn baby.”

While inside the elevator Amanda was staring Jenny down. “Which floor?” Amanda asked Derek.

“Top. What else?” Derek smiled.

The lift came to a rest. The doors opened exposing a very strange world, certainly foreign to Jenny. The room looked to be richly decorated; however, the visibility was limited due to a very high degree of low-key lighting.

“Over this way, girls,” yelled Derek.

Amanda and Jenny were soon joined by Joco and his associates.

“Good evening, sir,” said Derek. “I’d like you to meet a couple of friends. This is Amanda and Jenny.”

“Ladies,” Joco said, “won’t you come fly with me?”

Joco took a hit off his crack pipe then handed it to Amanda, who immediately joined in the celebration. "And now it was Jenny's turn. Here!" said Amanda, passing the dope over to her nervous friend. "Go ahead, you'll love it. Jenny took a drag. Now! Hold it in," ordered Amanda.

Jenny was choking. "What do you see in this?" she asked.

"You really want to know?" said Amanda. "I can produce a great sexual high alone, without surrendering my passions to some single-minded boy who will only use them to his own selfish end and forget my name in the process."

CHAPTER 11

Lisa and Dominic were back on the job and had been for quite a while, ever since leaving Dominic's apartment. It had been a long and extremely quiet ride.

Lisa seemed very uneasy and at odds with herself, torn between any good reporter's natural curiosity for a great story and her strong feelings of intimidation she got in spades from that almost iconic cop sitting to her extreme left. After much careful deliberation she finally decided to break down the wall of ice that had been building up between them ever since Stillwell's office.

"Back there Charley's wife, Irene, said something that's stuck in my mind. Your son and daughter-in-law. What happened? Care to share that?"

Dominic had always been a very private man, especially when it came to family. He had kept them and their memories alive only in the thoughts he sometimes shared with Maria. Perhaps it wouldn't hurt to let some of the pain out.

"Off the record?" he asked.

"You got it," she answered.

"My son, Jerry, was also an officer. Three years ago or better he and his wife, Chris, were both murdered in a car bombing."

"Did they ever find out who or why?" asked Lisa.

"You mean did he have any enemies? All good cops have those. But not this time. It was my car. It was meant for me all right and I know who's responsible."

"Who? And why didn't you arrest them?"

"Because they were up to their three-hundred-dollar shirt sleeves in big-time legal muscle."

"Now I begin to get the whole picture. It's this what's his name, Joco." Said Lisa. "Sure, it figures. Career officer set for retirement with honors picks up what's left of his family, Maria, and transfers out west to Los Angeles."

"You guess pretty damn good," said Dominic.

A low-rider car took a corner just opposite of Dominic and Lisa and slowly moved towards them.

"So what makes you think you can do here what you couldn't do in your own back yard?" asked Lisa.

"It'll happen, I'm a patient man. I'll either get him or they'll get…."

The strange car interrupted their interview, opening fire on Dominic, catching his right rear quarter panel. Dominic hit the lowest gear possible and peeled out in his supercharged eight, leaving the assassins behind. He was now headed for a more vacant neighborhood.

Suddenly from an alley the strike car reappeared and again fired. Dominic was jockeying his car back and forth to avoid any direct hits. During the chase, while his assailants were reloading, he seized the opportunity to get off a round or two himself. Pulling his 38 and pointing to his right, he found Lisa in direct line of fire.

"Get the hell down!" he yelled.

She was glaring to her left only to be met by a loaded handgun staring her in the face. She immediately obeyed. Two rounds were more than enough to kill the main gunman and force his fellow outlaws to a slow and abrupt halt. Dominic spun his car around a complete 180 degrees some 50 yards away. Looking down the now deserted street all that was in his sights was the lone attack vehicle. Without a beat he hit the gas with all of his weight and off they went, headed directly towards the other car, which by this time had a pretty damn good idea of what Dominic had in store for it.

"That pig is one crazy mother fucker. Let's book man," said one gang member.

Lisa rose up in relief only to panic once again at the hands of still another one of Pisa's crazy ideas. Her look was worth a thousand words. He was now obsessed and with his customary tunnel vision, pressed straight on towards the other car.

"This prick is out to kill us all," said another gangster. "Hit it!"

Both cars were now and again well under way but only one driver had any thoughts at all of trying to avoid permanent harm's way. Seconds later, trying to negate a point of full-on impact, the gang swerved quickly to their right, hitting a small lumber stack in the process which was more than enough to launch them forward and aft into a very large and solid iron, 40-yard industrial waste bin, exploding their car on impact.

Dominic skidded to a stop, jumped out armed and ready, walked slowly towards the blaze of burning flesh. He yelled through the smoke and flames, "Joco will be along shortly. Till then you all have the right to remain silent!"

A few beats later Lisa was able to eject herself from their somewhat bullet-ridden car.

"You all right?" asked Dominic.

"No thanks to you, you crazy, irresponsible bastard! You almost got us killed! That could have possibly been us in there. Well maybe you have a death wish, officer, but I'm young and would like to kind of keep it that way. And if I do go prematurely, it won't be at the hands of some throwback from the middle ages who walks and talks like an old Raymond Chandler novel."

"Well of all the ungrateful...... I think you're missing the point here," pointing to the wreckage, "they came after us. Just a clear case of survival."

CHAPTER 12

Some time had passed but all present at Joco's were still smoking on the joy pipe with the exception of a few weaker souls satisfied to rest and enjoy the moment. Not so for Amanda. It seemed that his honor's heiress was about to dig herself and her young companion an even deeper hole. Joco was glaring at Amanda.

"Baby, you can really go. I like that in a woman. You are a woman?" he asked.

"What is that supposed to mean?" she answered.

"I mean are you woman enough?"

"For what?" she answered.

"Woman enough for a little brown sugar?" said Joco while stroking her hair.

"I've never been with a black man," answered Amanda.

"You try black, you never go back."

"That's not what we came for," said Amanda, pulling away.

Joco still holding her tightly, "when you come to Joco's, Sis, you come for it all."

Jenny was becoming extremely scared. "Mandy," she said, "let's go."

"Derek!" ordered Amanda, "We would like to leave."

Young Derek looked over to his ruthless boss while placing his arms firmly around Jenny, "When the man says!"

Joco grabbed Amanda, pulling her head and face to his, "And the man ain't said!"

Jenny began to panic. "Please don't do this," she pleaded. Jenny screamed and pulled with all her strength away from Derek's vice-like grip, only to fall backwards through the full-length window sheers over the balcony and 20 stories down to a horrible death.

Amanda could not believe her eyes.

"Take care of that," said Joco to Tyrone, "and see that we are not disturbed."

Every woman's absolute nightmare, young or old was about to come calling on our young socialite. The ultimate physical and mental violation. Joco and his partners, Derek included, assaulted and raped young Amanda Parks repeatedly.

CHAPTER 13

WKLP for an independent TV station and one that possessed countless awards for journalism around the world had still maintained a surprisingly casual approach in its presentation. It started its day with anything but a normal show, it was filled with laughter. You, the audience, got the genuine feeling of family that these people, the weather guy, the anchor boy and girl, and the rapid-fire entertainment editor not only had to be there each and every good day L.A. – but they all really liked being up at that ungodly hour, and they most certainly enjoyed each other. Their viewers did not come away with that straightforward monotonous dialog you seemed to receive tuning into, shall we say, the networks. Perhaps this is why Lisa Powers chose this unusual station to establish her own career.

Today, the day after her near miss at the hands of dirty Dominic, as she had newly christened Lieutenant Pisa, she was sitting at her word processor punching in last night's events. She was interrupted by her boss, Bill Curtis, who was spying over her shoulder trying to sneak a peek.

"Are we onto something here?" he asked.

"Do me a favor will you, Bill? The next time I get any noble thoughts about saving anything, especially this town, put your foot where it will get my most undivided attention."

"Having second thoughts, are we?"

"Second, third, and you name it. Whatever I get out of this will be, believe me, well earned."

"That bad, huh?" said Bill.

"Worse," said Lisa. "I've met some pretty difficult individuals in this job, who hasn't. It plays a big part, but your lieutenant is the most narrow-minded, self-centered, egotistical, trigger-happy, public servant it has ever been my displeasure to meet."

"Well, I'll be. I hear his fellow officers swear by him," said Bill.

"Are you sure that wasn't swear at?"

"Anyway, when did he get to be my lieutenant?" said Bill. "Holler when you've had enough."

It was 5 o'clock that same day. Dominic had just gotten an urgent call from one of his ace rats, a necessary evil cops sometimes aligned themselves with to get underground street information in order to catch some person or persons who had really stepped over the line.

Manny Limo was just like any other low-life, only a little more so. He'd especially sell or sell out anything or anybody for a buck or two. He was the poster boy for every guy your mother's warned you about growing up. Short, skinny to a fault, pock-marked, with his always shiny and oily white-bar pallor complexion, not exactly your average white-collar ad, but what he lacked in obvious physical beauty he made up with in cunning. Manny was going to get his way whether it was a beautiful woman he had to have or just a smash-and-grab fast cash takedown, no matter what the risk. You never found those types uptown, generally they preferred to seek their own levels somewhere down and dirty. They all seemed to float to the top along with the rest of the shit!

Dominic had called Lisa to meet him at Manny's place, a rundown diner on 7th and L.A. Street. He was cutting his way past through the homeless that incorporated this section of skid row, the end of the line for all down-and-outers on the bum, with an occasional over-the-hill prostitute passing by here and there trying to do their level best with whatever they had left. Dominic entered the beat up and beat down, cockroach-infested eatery that was Limo's dismal front. He was met by a contrary Lisa Powers.

"Lovely place, Lieutenant. Come here often? What made you choose this spot? The colorful mixture of Americana?" she asked.

"The coffee's hot and the tips are right out of the fucking horse's mouth. You're probably used to Laury's Prime Rib."

Out through the bare-bulb lighting and illegal cigarette smoke appeared Manny.

"Evening, Lieutenant," he said. "Got something for you."

Dominic looked up while sipping the coffee cup he had just wiped down, "Speak of the devil and he shows up."

"And it's hot, sir," said Manny, "real hot."

"Better be, punk. I'm busy and I'm off to a shit day. Gimme."

"Maybe we should discuss price?" said Manny.

Dominic grabbed Manny by his ragged tie, "Or maybe I should just kick your worthless ass!"

"Take it easy, Pap. I got this friend that works at Superior Memorial. Seems early this morning they bring in this young girl or what's left of her."

"So why tell me?" asked Dominic.

"So they got her listed as a Jane Doe."

Dominic tightened his grip, "I hope to God for your sake this has a wow finish, scum bag."

"My friend thinks this is a little odd," said Manny, trying desperately to talk with half his windpipe sealed off. "So he starts doing a little checking. Turns out she's the daughter of some high-powered legal stiff."

"Again, why me? City's full of them!" he yelled.

"Because this particular stiff has been a special pain in your ass since you hit this town."

Dominic tightened even more.

"Parks, Manville Parks!"

"Couldn't happen to a nicer guy."

Manny now was really fighting for each breath. Dominic released his grip, "You did good kid! Real good. That's one I owe you."

"Owe?" asked a disappointed and frightened Manny.

"You'll get what's coming to you, I guarantee it!" said Dominic, walking out the door with his now somewhat reluctant passenger.

"You're not only crude, Lieutenant, you're positively barbaric. That poor man," said Lisa.

"That poor man's been a professional criminal ever since he got something for nothing. Hard work is not in his vocabulary. He's a 2-time loser for rape and child abuse. He's goddamn lucky he's not dead or mutilated. Maybe you'd like to meet him. I can hook you up!"

Lisa ignored the last part. "Was he talking about the Manville Parks?"

"You mean there's two or more of that asshole on the bench?"

"I know him socially through my uncle. He is one of a handful of the most respected legal giants in the country."

"Respected by who? Not by me," said Dominic.

"Well the governor for one, and about 200 of this state's most influential special interests are giving him a dinner next month," said Lisa.

"Sort of in His Honor's honor," said Dominic.

"Why do you hate him so?" Lisa asked.

"It's a little game we play, the good judge and me. I catch the bastards red-handed and he turns them loose."

"Why would he?" asked Lisa.

"I have a theory. Remember last evening before we were so interrupted by the Uzi Four? I was about to speak of my gut feeling. There exists in this country a drug council and it controls all the drug traffic coast to coast. Guys like Joco are only pawns in the biggest chess game in town."

"What's all this got to do with a man like Judge Parks?" she asked.

"He's a charter member and God knows how many others with his power and clout. How the hell else do you think these drug lords stay in business? And I'm talking billions of tax-free money and strictly cash. With that kind of wealth you can control anything and corrupt anybody."

"That is an incredible theory Lieutenant. If you could prove that it would set this town that has seen, heard and survived nearly everything, right on its glamorous ear."

"I can't prove it! Not yet anyway," said Dominic. "But I'll make book that Parks for sure is in this right up to his fucking Rolex. Let's go."

CHAPTER 14

Superior Memorial Hospital was far removed from the stark, noisy, overcrowded and desperate conditions over at County. Its halls bespoke the wealth and aristocracy of its guests. Dominic and Lisa had just presented their valuable identifications to the head nurse. Nurse Martin looked for all the world just like one would expect in her position, a no-nonsense attitude with an extremely official persona, able to deal with any and all situations. She had done her absolute best to hide any signs of femininity, horn-rimmed glasses, hair pulled back as tight as allowed, and the swagger of an upright and uptight lady trucker.

“How may I help you?” she asked.

“A few hours ago your people brought in a young girl. A rape victim,” said Dominic. “We’d like to see her. It’s my belief she is listed under a Jane Doe.”

“That’s impossible. I have been on for several hours and no one has been admitted with that description,” said the nurse.

“Get me the head of admitting,” said Dominic.

“That would be Mrs. Hutchinson.”

“Well go get her and now!” he ordered.

Lisa gave him a sour look.

“Please,” he added.

A few moments passed and in the distance a very slight figure appeared.

"I'm Mrs. Hutchinson, Lieutenant. What is it?" she asked.

"We're looking for a young girl about sixteen."

"Extremely pretty," Lisa interjected.

"She has been attacked. It's very critical that we see her. It's part of an ongoing investigation."

Mrs. Hutchinson hesitated. Dominic was staring down both of the older women. "I don't understand your hesitation, ladies. If you know anything, let's have it."

"Tell him!" said Nurse Martin to the other woman.

"I'm very sorry officer; it's just that they said not to release a thing, especially to the press."

"She's with me and it's off the record," said Dominic referring to Lisa.

"What do you mean? Off what record, yours or mine?" Lisa said while butting in.

"I assure you both, Miss Powers and I will be the very essence of discretion and I haven't used a phrase that big in years. Now shall we?" Dominic and Lisa, along with the two ladies had taken the elevator way to the top reserved for special patients and their associates.

"You know, Mrs. Hutchinson, when you find out who they are you'll never have need for a shrink. Ha!" he laughed.

The ladies were not sharing in his laughter or in his cavalier attitude. The elevator stopped at the very top floor, home to the VIP medical suites. Dominic and Lisa were met by Judge Park's chief assistant, Carl Smithers.

Smithers extended his hand which seemed to be ignored completely by Dominic. "I'm Carl Smithers,

Lieutenant. I am sure you can appreciate the levity of the situation."

"I know who you are," answered Dominic. "Where's the girl?"

"This is her private physician, Dr. Benjamin Hoffman, Lieutenant." Acknowledging the doctor, "Doctor. this is Miss Powers."

"What are we looking at here?" asked Dominic.

"A very sick young woman. She has been through an incredible physical and mental abusive ordeal."

"What are her chances, doc?"

"Physically fair, but mentally we are light years away."

"Can we see her?" asked Lisa.

"I have her under heavy sedation."

"They told me downstairs the family was here," said Dominic.

"I can answer any questions you might have, Lieutenant," said Smithers.

"Perhaps you didn't hear me," said the doctor. "Miss Parks has had a severe mental breakdown. I can't promise you a thing."

"What else is new?" said Dominic, heading for the high-speed elevator.

"Will you answer me one thing, Pisa?" asked Lisa, "what the hell did we accomplish in there?"

"Not a damn thing for now!"

"Then why?"

"When somebody tries to cover up – it pushes against my cop instincts."

"I would think it obvious why the family handled things the way they did," said Lisa. "A prominent judge, very powerful in this state, his only daughter, practically a baby, is raped repeatedly and God knows what else. What good would any publicity serve?"

"I can understand the private angle. What bothers my piece of mind are the events before and after the attack, in your vernacular, Miss Powers, who, what, where, when and how."

"You're not suggesting they are withholding anything."

"You bet your sweet laptop. The only reason we showed up here tonight was to flush out a rat, maybe two. Somebody in that tidy group may panic and when that happens I want to be there so I can step on their tail."

"I don't understand any of this," said Lisa.

"Just sit back, take your notes and enjoy the ride," said Dominic.

"I've already had my share of the ride and you can keep it."

Suddenly Dominic's radio went off. It's the dispatcher. One 700 – see the man – Landmark Hotel, Aviation and Century Blvd., room 540, possible 187. Respond. Do you read?

He grabbed the mike, "One 700 – Roger that. I copy, will respond. You copy, Helen?" he asked.

"I copy."

“What’s a 187?” asked Lisa. “Sounds pretty critical.”

“Some more than others. Sure you want to come? It could get messy, 187 is homicide.”

CHAPTER 15

Room 540 was busier than the honeymoon suites. The room was filled with police officers and homicide CSI crowded around the bludgeoned corpse of the young, pretty, red-headed call girl. They all were going about with pains-taking precision scraping DNA samples from virtually everywhere, furniture, wall moulding, picking up hair fragments, looking for anything that could give them a leg up on the killer.

Dominic and Lisa had joined the hunting party. This would be Lisa's first dead body, up close, but certainly not to be her last contact with violent death first hand.

"My God, she looks so young. Who could of done this? What sort of sick mind?"

"I told you it could get messy," Said Dominic.

"You see this every day?" asked Lisa.

"This and worse in the Apple for twenty years before I switched to vice. But it's all the same, killer or pusher; a scum bag is a scum bag."

"Dom, to what do we owe the honor of your presence?" asked a passing officer. "Slumming? This is a homicide."

"I can see that Turner," said Dominic. "Possibly our girl here might just be working. That makes it my play. You got a problem with that?"

"Take it easy, Pap, just curious."

"Well, curiosity killed the cat."

"You mean she was a prostitute?" asked Lisa. "But why kill her?"

"Why? Lady, I stopped asking that question thirty years ago. How the hell do I or anybody know what goes on in the mind of a man that would do this? What kind of rage? Maybe his mother or father kicked his ass too many times or maybe he asked too many questions. He obviously has got a hard on for the working class. Chet, I want a copy of your team's findings ASAP. Okay buddy? Maybe this will tie in."

"You got it Dom," said Chet.

"What results?" Lisa asked.

"Whether or not this kid was a user. Most are. Did she have sex with her assailant? Was she on the needle? Will she test positive? A lot of variables. If we know she was on drugs, I might can get a line on her supplier. With that I can trace him back to this hotel for a possible contact or pimp, if you prefer."

"Why not check the desk to see who was staying here?" asked Lisa.

"Too easy. This guy is a hell of a lot smarter than that. I'll bet you a dinner at Laury's there was no one registered."

"Right again," said Chet passing by.

"Find out who was tending bar tonight. I want to talk to them."

"Well it's late, let's call it night paisan," said Chet. "Pleasure Ms. Powers. Do call again."

"But not too soon, Sergeant," answered Lisa.

“Where the fuck does that old Dago get off trying to tell us our job?” said Turner to Chet Higgins.

“That old Dago is a dying breed. A cop’s cop, and he happens to be my personal hero, so shut the fuck up!” said Chet.

CHAPTER 16

Dominic, while making his way towards his apartment was met by Maria's sitter and their neighbor, Mrs. Cooper.

Beth Cooper was a woman in her late seventies. She had about ten years on Dominic. Lost her husband of fifty-eight years to Alzheimer's two years ago. They had met while they both served in the Korean Conflict. Her husband got a Medal of Honor at Chosin Reservoir with the Marines and their famous march to the sea.

"I just looked in on her again, Mr. Pisa. She's doing just fine, sleeping like a newborn."

"Thank you, ma'am and have a good night. See you tomorrow evening."

He entered his apartment, tossed down his keys and made a straight line for the scotch. He poured himself a tall one neat and then flopped into a nearby chair. In his search for a much needed last smoke of the day, he came across the family album. While thumbing through its pages full of lost loved ones his tough exterior began to fade. What remained was just a man, a man whose family ties ran incredibly deep. Tears welled up in this old soldier's eyes. The moment was fortified when Maria joined him crying.

"I miss them too, Papa," she said, trying to comfort him.

"I know, honey, I know."

Lisa had just stepped off the penthouse elevator at the Doheny Regency, a wealthy, high-end own-your-own apartment building just off the Sunset Strip. The elevator lead directly into her richly decorated living area. The rooms were dark except for a full moon shining through. A figure casts a silhouette against a white wall. Her fear began to swell as she reached for her mace with one hand and a light switch with the other, flicking on the lights at the ready.

"It's about time you got home!" said Bill Curtis. "You know, Lisa, if we are to continue these romantic liaisons you're going to have to keep better hours."

"Do I detect a small measure of jealousy, Mr. Curtis?"

"You had better believe it. I'm jealous of anything or anybody who monopolizes your time."

"Well a girl has to make a living."

"That's a laugh," said Bill. "Honey, you could buy and sell half of the power brokers you write about."

"You know my career, Bill, has never had anything to do with money or power. It's critical to me to be appreciated for what I am and what I do, not for my last name or for a healthy bank balance or bottom line, my dear Mr. Curtis, that I just happen to sleep with the boss."

"I particularly like that last part," said Bill, pulling Lisa tightly against his body.

Lisa looked deep into his eyes. He gently stroked her face, outlining her lips with his index finger just before they kissed. They both could sense immediately a heavy level of passion as he accelerated his movements, massaging her now perky breasts to a point of no return.

Their breathing soared with the anticipation of things to come.

Bill picked her up and snagged a pair of crystal flutes and a vintage bottle he had standing by and off they went to do what all young practicing heterosexuals do best.

CHAPTER 17

Dominic had come to work a bit early to pick up the tapes from the night of the bust and to review the preliminary findings on the dead girl. He, along with Chet Higgins and a few other detectives had joined Captain Stillwell in a conference room.

"Well, let's have it gentlemen," said Stillwell. "What have we got on this latest killing?"

"Young woman approximately 25 years of age, 5 feet 5 inches tall, 110 pounds, brown hair, blue eyes. Initial cause of death, according to the ME, broken neck," answered Chet.

"Wait a minute, what the hell do you mean initial?" asked Stillwell.

"She was also bludgeoned."

"She was beaten up after she was dead?"

"Yes sir, Captain," said Chet. "Just like the others."

"Others?" asked Stillwell. "There are more? Tell me we don't have a serial nut case out there on my watch."

"He's killing young, pretty, even beautiful, young hookers. Six to date."

"Fuck!" yelled Stillwell. "What do we have? Any leads?"

"Nothing as yet, sir," answered Chet.

"Well, guys, it's way too thin. We have got to get something and fast, so I'll lay this down only once. We are going to work around-the-clock starting tonight. If any of you've got plans, forget it! I want everyone this department knows questioned, every pimp, hustler, sex offender, mob connections to prostitution, massage parlors, escort bureaus, you name it. There will be no sacred cows on this one. This fucker is the real deal. Now I'm assigning Dominic here to you, Chet, and your people. His extensive background in homicide should be invaluable."

"Wait a minute! Captain, I've got a prior commitment. Besides, what about Ms. Powers?" he asked.

"Take her along. She might find homicide more newsworthy. Your other case can be put on hold. That pusher is not going anywhere. That's all gentlemen. Pap, wait here, I want to talk with you."

Everyone else began filtering out mumbling their individual reactions to what just went down.

"Pap, what do I do with you?" scolded Stillwell. "You're obviously too old to spank!"

"What's your point Captain?"

"Ms. Powers' safety is of top priority here and I don't want you to lose sight of that."

"I know things got a little shaky the other night, Boss, but that wasn't my fault."

"Then what the hell do you call a high-speed chase with four dead?" asked Stillwell.

Dominic thinking, self defense.

"Get out of here! And another thing, stay away from that judge and his family. That's an order!"

"We will handle it," said Officers Jackson and Turner, standing next to Stillwell's office.

“Great! I’ll rest a lot better knowing that,” quipped Dominic.

“And none of your smart ass, Pap,” said Stillwell.

“Do I get Johnnie’s tapes or not?” asked Dominic.

“Try the property room. Might be a good start.”

“Sure Boss,” said Dominic while walking away mumbling to himself that smart ass works both ways.

On his way to the property warehouse Dominic passed Detective Harve Bennett’s office, who had just hung up his hard line.

“How do you like that bitch! I’m trying to help and she cops an attitude.”

“Yeah!” said Dominic. “The general public can be a little difficult at times.”

“Bull shit! Nothing general or public about this gal, not with a Bel Air address.”

Bel Air, why do I, thought Dominic. “What address?”

“Two thousand block, big time old money,” answered Harve.

“What’s the complaint?” asked Dominic.

“No complaint, possibly missing person.”

“Let me see that,” said Dominic. Jenny Baker, he read.

“Do you know this kid?” asked Harve.

“Just a theory, pal.”

“Well, you can have it, Pap.”

"What's up, Harve, you got something against money?"

"Only those who didn't earn it!" answered Harve.

"Well, I got news, I've been working my ass off since I was fourteen and they haven't missed a fucking thing. Something else, when Lisa Powers checks in tell her I'll be at this address," said Dominic passing a note while walking away.

Dominic's mood was definitely on the upswing. Armed with the possible break he had just gotten from Bennett, there was even a skip to his walk as he headed down the stairs leading to the property room where he was met by a white-haired officer named Gino.

"You know why I like you so much, Gino?" asked Dominic. "It's not because your last name ends in a vowel, but you're the only guy in this whole damned department that's old enough to remember what the hell he was doing the year I was born."

"So why are a couple of old horses like us still around?" asked Gino.

"Where else you gonna find a job that pays this good and has all the physical security to boot," answered Dominic.

Before he could finish his sarcasm a disturbance had broken out in one of the holding cells adjacent to property.

"What the hell was that?" asked Dominic.

"Better check it out, Pap. I'll be right along."

Dominic rounded a corner following the bellowing sounds of a young black prisoner being beaten by a burly white officer and his solid hickory nightstick. Apparently the boy had been cuffed to the bars and struck repeatedly.

Dominic clasped his hands together on the run and swung with everything he had, blind siding the assailing officer, knocking the overweight uniformed man off his feet.

Once down, Dominic did what any good New Yorker in a fit of rage would do. He worked him over, this man half his age.

"You dirty, rotten son-of-a-bitch. How the hell did you ever get on this man's force?" yelled Dominic.

Gino tried his best to calm his fellow Italian down. "Stop Dominic! You're killing him!"

"What the fuck do you think this prick was trying to do to this kid? If it's my last act, I'll have your badge and pension. You put a stink on every good man who ever wore a shield.

CHAPTER 18

It was mid-afternoon on a school day. That meant only one thing to a kid just beginning their twelve year stretch of schooling. It was time to leave, go home, see and talk to your friends or just plain make new ones.

Lisa Powers had been waiting and watching for Maria Pisa from her expensive Italian car. Her instincts as a reporter told her what better way to know a man like Lieutenant Pisa than to talk to his only living relative. Maybe this young girl could give her a little much needed insight into this complicated human being, she thought. Suddenly she spotted the 9-year-old talking to a boy. She pulled her car over to the curb alongside Maria.

"Can I give you a ride home, young lady?"

Maria was staring her down, "Lisa, right?" she asked.

"Maria, right?" answered Lisa.

"Sure," said Maria laughingly, "why not. I could skip two grades waiting for the bus. You know, Lisa," said Maria climbing into the low-slung sports car, "You can't be too careful these days. Lots of nuts out there grabbing kids."

"I'll say. Not to change the subject, but who was that heartthrob I saw you talking to?"

"You mean Danny?" answered Maria looking back at the boy. "He is cute but still and all a boy."

"Don't tell me you like the older guys," said Lisa.

"Papa always said that when I pick a man to go for the more mature type."

"You mean like Brad Pitt?"

"Yeah! He's great."

"He also has a famous wife and more than a few children."

"Are you sure?" asked Maria.

"It's my business to know these things."

"How is it going working alongside my Papa? He can be more than difficult at times, you know, but you just have to sense how to get around him."

"What's your secret?" Lisa asked.

"Well with Italians, especially the older generation of men, you have to let them think everything is their idea, that you are going to do it their way. Then when it comes down to it, you do it yours. Simple."

"Nothing is that simple, least wise not with that gentleman."

"You gonna see him again tonight?" Maria asked.

"Right after I let you off I've got to meet him at some home on the west side."

"What's that all about?"

"Don't know," answered Lisa. "Say, I'm the reporter here. I will ask all the questions."

"Turn right up here and we're the second building on the left. Thanks Lisa. Hope to see a lot more of you."

"Me too, Maria. Here's my card. Call me anytime; we'll have a real sit down girl talk."

Like any metropolitan city, Los Angeles had its beautiful areas. Her skyline had certainly changed from the days when City Hall was the tallest and most striking building in town. Today it is dwarfed by the high rise walls of glass that now incorporate its busy downtown boundaries. Gone are the old superb stately mansions that lived on Bunker Hill. Today in their once peaceful bedroom neighborhoods resided countless lofts, both old and new, complete with their own ground floor commercial flats selling just about any and all merchandise.

However, some areas never change, or in this case the founding father's fathers hadn't gotten around to cleaning up, all those embarrassing spots that most important towns try to ignore. If they don't see it on a daily basis, it doesn't exist, or maybe it will go away on its own. They're not the perfect picture you're apt to see in the Sunday travel section of your favorite newspaper. There are endless alleyways full of lost souls in life that have all for the most part resigned themselves to life on the streets and its survival of the fittest attitude.

The alley in particular that day was the home to a dozen or so sweet losers who had all gathered together to share in the dangerous game of injecting cocaine. A man and woman had just finished and were about to pass on their fix kit to the next customer. But before doing so the needle must be cleaned. There was no available water. A father quickly reached down and retrieved his young son's baby bottle. All the rest quietly sat nearby observing this crude, suicidal process. Still another addict who was bored waiting for his turn decided to cross over to a nearby seven-yard, insect-ridden, filthy dumpster to fish through its contents for anything of value. The catch that day was more than anyone could have bargained for. There in lied the mortal remains of one Jenny Baxter.

CHAPTER 19

The Baxter mansion was just what you would expect from a self-made man, Harvey Baxter. He didn't go to USC Law School like his prominent neighbor, Judge Manville Parks. He didn't even go to college. High school was more than he or his school could handle. Ever since he was a kid playing along with his young companions at his father's radiator shop off Manchester and Broadway, he had enjoyed working on automobiles, the older the better. He had just the right knack for fixing anything mechanical.

He knocked around from shop to shop until one day some well-to-do fancy pants walked into one of the joints Harvey was working and took an immediate liking to the youngster and the brilliant rapport he had with most reciprocating engines.

"How could I get more horsepower out of this stock engine of mine, Kid?" he asked.

Well, Harvey took a look at his carburetor and said, "There's your problem. It's not allowing enough gas up into the right spot, consequently there won't be enough spark to get the right explosion at the right time. Now if we could come up with an electronic system that would work faster your car would go faster."

"How much do you need?" asked the stranger.

"Probably 100,000 dollars to start. It's a lot of money, I know, but it'll take a lot of time and effort."

Well six months and 150,000 dollars later the electronic ignition system was born. They sold the idea, but kept the patents, to General Motors for several million dollars. And that brings us up-to-date on all three Baxters.

Dominic had just arrived at the Baxter residence in Brentwood where he was met by the ever impatient Lisa. "I'll bet you're late for your own memorial service," she said.

"Before we ring the bell I have something to share," said Dominic. "The case I was on got put on hold. You and I are now working last night's homicide. Stillwell feels Chet and the boys need help, just until they get something concrete."

"Then why, Lieutenant, are we here?" she asked.

"We're not," said Dominic ringing the bell.

The door opened promptly. Dominic and Lisa were both greeted by Jenny's solemn parents.

Mrs. Baxter was crying.

"This is not at all like our daughter to go out and not come home without a call. She always calls Lieutenant," said Harvey Baxter, "I don't think we have to convince you of our concern. You're probably a parent yourself."

"Yes, sir," replied Dominic feeling that same old devastating pain. "Did your daughter say where she was going and with who?" he asked.

"Just a girlfriend," Mrs. Baxter replied.

"Good. What was her name?"

"Oh, dear, just one of the girls from school. I believe her name was Sandy or Sandra something like that. I can't remember."

"I'm going to need to take a look at her cell phone's recent records. You probably pay her bill?"

"Yes, of course we do," answered Mr. Baxter. "What's the second thing?" he asked.

"I'd like to see her laptop computer. I assume she has one in her room."

"Of course, right this way," said Mrs. Baxter.

While she and Lisa went ahead, Harvey Baxter purposely hung back with Dominic.

"How does it look Lieutenant? Do you think this might be a kidnapping? I'm extremely wealthy."

"Can't say for sure. We just got the report. How long has she been missing?" asked Dominic.

"Since the last two evenings."

"Mr. and Mrs. Baxter, I'm sorry I haven't introduced my assistant, Ms. Lisa Powers. She's the expert PC gal. I'm a little old school."

"Pleasure," said the Baxters. Here is Jenny's room."

"Do you mind if I have a look around while Lisa probes her internet, checks her My Space for pictures or correspondence, recent e-mails, that sort of thing?"

Dominic was scanning the room. "Do you have a picture of her in the outfit she went out in, or could you describe it?"

"It was a red dress, knee length. She never dressed cheap."

"Any identifying marks, birth, scars as a kid, or maybe even a tattoo?"

"Of course not," replied Mrs. Baxter. "We wouldn't allow her defacing herself. She has beautiful skin."

"Did the red dress have an off the shoulder top?" asked Lisa, bringing up Jenny's My Space.

"Why yes, I believe so."

"Is this her in the dress?"

"That's it. You've got it Miss Powers," answered Mrs. Baxter.

"Stay with it, Lisa," said Dominic. "See if she has any recent shots of her friends."

"We haven't been here but a few months," said Harvey Baxter.

"What's this group picture, is it recent?" Lisa asked.

Mrs. Baxter was studying the photo, "Yes, that's recent because the statue they're all sitting on is the front of Merridithy, an exclusive high school for girls. They must have taken it with Jenny's cell phone or someone else's camera."

"Out of those six girls in the picture do you recognize any of them as the girl your daughter was last seen with?"

Mrs. Baxter put on her reading glasses and took a good look. "That one in the back row center, I think. Yes, I believe that's her."

"Lisa can separate that girl and enlarge her. Yes, that's it. Now can we print a copy of the entire photo along with the enlarged one of the girl?" Dominic asked.

"Sure, it will only take a minute," Lisa said.

"She's a pretty girl. They both are almost striking. Could that girl's name be something like Mandy or Amanda?" he asked.

"Please Lieutenant, if you know something, anything!" said Mr. Baxter.

"It's just a hunch, but she could be Amanda Parks. It would figure. This girl lives less than a block away and her father is Manville Parks, a very prominent judge. She's a pretty wild kid."

Dominic's phone went off. "Sorry, I have to take this in private. I'll be right back. Yeah! Pisa here. What you got Bennett?"

Pausing, "Yeah, Pap. I got something but I don't think you're going to like it," replied Bennett.

"How bad?" asked Dominic.

"They just pulled a body out of a trash heap over off of 9th and San Pedro. Could be that young Baxter girl. Does she have a red dress on? Looks like it was red, can't tell what with all the blood loss."

"Cause of death?" asked Dominic.

"Preliminary? Blunt impact, my guess like she fell from a great height," said Bennett.

"Where is she now?" asked Dominic.

"Coroner's got her. We might have to go with the DNA or even dental."

"I'm on my way. Thanks Bennett for the heads up."

"Anything for you, Pap," Bennett said.

Dominic rejoined Lisa and the Baxters. "Could we borrow Jenny's computer folks?" he asked.

"Certainly, anything you and your assistant might need, Lieutenant," said Mr. Baxter.

"Thank you," said Mrs. Baxter, "and may god bless you both."

"Thank you, Ma'am. We can all use any help we can get."

A late model limousine pulled up to an exclusive English Tudor apartment building built back in the 20's, The Park Manor. Two extremely well-dressed people got out. An older gentleman in his 60's with grey, thinning hair escorted his beautiful, young female companion to the entrance.

"I had a marvelous time," said the man, "you're as good as you look!"

"And you're as rich as they said."

"Richer!" he said. "Here's a little extra. Shall I see you in?"

"That won't be necessary, Paul. I enjoyed you on all levels. Please call me again."

"I can't think of anything I'd like better. Good night my dear."

They kissed. He left and retreated back to his car and off she went like Marilyn Monroe walking down the train in "Some Like it Hot", great ass and all. She immediately began searching her expensive handbag for her keys as she walked along the tree-lined path to her bungalow. She heard a strange voice.

"So you had a good time, why was that?" asked the mystery voice.

"I beg your pardon? Who's there?" she asked.

"I'm an admirer. Over this way."

Before the young woman's self-preservation button could sound, curiosity had led her directly towards the almost hypnotic voice.

"Are we neighbors?" she asked.

Suddenly without warning a giant hand reached out through the heavy plant life and clasped over her pretty face. Her body left the ground almost immediately in a perfect vertical rise. Her struggles for life were silenced with a brief cracking sound. In one quick, violent movement another in a long line of premium ladies of comfort was silenced forever.

CHAPTER 20

Most city morgues were just what they appeared like in the movies, cold, dimly lit walls of stainless steel drawers containing countless corpses who had all recently met the reaper or the Angel of Death, be it grimly or otherwise.

Dominic and Lisa were passing by what seemed to be a sea of bodies on display, none yet ready to be placed in their own private sliding gurney.

"Maybe I should step out, Lieutenant. This is police business," said Lisa nervously.

"Step out? Oh no, Ms. Powers, I wouldn't think of it! This is critical police work."

They were met by the chief coroner, Dan Seltzer. "Pap," said Dan, "I know I'm not supposed to get personally involved in my work, I just can't help it. This kid with her whole life ahead makes one mistake and it's over."

"What mistake?" asked Dominic.

"Well, just a preliminary workup showed drugs and a high degree, but not from a prolonged use," said Dan.

"Cause of death?" asked Dominic.

"Death was instantaneous, caused by a severe impact, perhaps a fall from a great height."

"Any chance it could have been suicide or maybe she got stoned and just fell?"

"I don't buy it, Pap," said Dan. "Her dress was torn and she had bruises like she'd been held tightly against her will."

"Any guess as to the time of death?"

"Judging from the rigor I'd imagine around midnight."

"That would coincide with the Parks kid's bad luck," said Dominic to Lisa. "Dan, you've got a great shot at making my evening. Anything, hair follicles, skin fragments, semen, DNA from anywhere, blood breakdown, I really want the shit who was capable of this, okay? And ASAP."

"My pleasure. I've got teenage girls too. Get this guy or guys."

"Call me, Dan, when you got a positive ID, and anybody who might have been involved."

"That's the second time in my life I've seen violent death. I imagine you are used to it after 30 years," said Lisa.

"Anybody tells you they're used to it, including me," said Dominic, "and I'll show you a sick, insensitive mother fucker!"

"Sincerely put, Lieutenant, and thanks for sharing that."

"This is not the goddamn movies where the hero, with a name nobody can pronounce, kills 150 guys with his semi you know, Miss Powers," said Dominic "I'd just once like to hear the asshole at the end of the film say, 'hey you kids out there, don't try this at home.' How about a hot cup?" he asked, "by that time Dan should have a positive lead on the people that did this."

“That quick?” asked Lisa. “Modern police science, we’ve come a long way since latent prints.”

CHAPTER 21

The hard line at Joco's place was ringing off the hook. Tyrone finally picked up.

"Excuse me, sir, it's for you, Derek James."

Joco reluctantly took the receiver, "Yes Derek. What is it?"

"Sir, I'm worried about last night."

"No problem, man," said Joco, "what we had here was just a quiet get together. All the cops got is two teenage bimbos, one brain dead and the other one permanent, with no way in hell to trace them back here."

"If you say so, sir, I was just a little concerned," said Derek.

"Well son, don't be. We have business commitments to consider. Now then, listen to what I tell you. Tyrone will pick you up in exactly one hour. I want you to go to the Bonaventure Hotel and pick up a package at the desk addressed to you. Got it?" he asked. "Tyrone will have further orders."

"Yes sir!" assured Derek. "A package addressed to me. Got it, sir, and I'm real sorry I sounded so negative."

"Don't give it another thought," said Joco.

Jad's Coffee Shop was just a short hike from the ME's office and the morgue. Everything as fresh as can be and the coffee was always hot with one brewing and one pouring. It got its simple name from the owners, a couple of Armenians, John and Demetri. The food tasted as if it were prepared by the best cook from any American household. Prices were reasonable and the place was tastefully decorated with a homey touch. Occasionally Jad's let the bill slide for LA's finest. Hopefully no idiot was apt to pull anything stupid while they were up to their crooked ass in heat.

Lisa and Dominic had already been waiting word.

"Do you mind if I ask a personal question?"

"Go ahead, as long as it's not too personal," joked Dominic. "Besides you probably would anyway."

"Don't you think Maria is a big responsibility for a man your age?" asked Lisa.

"Oh! I get it, I'm certainly old enough to have insane gang members shoot at me but just a little long in the tooth for parenthood."

"Well, what I really meant was why couldn't you leave her with another member of the family? Preferably a female," asked Lisa.

"I got custody because she had nobody else. My son, Jerry, and his wife, Chris, were both only children. My wife and my daughter-in-law's parents are also gone. Sound a little like your favorite soap? I had two things going for me, I'm her only blood relative." There was a pause in his speech.

"You said two," pressed Lisa.

"And I love that little girl as much as anyone could love," answered Dominic.

"Then why do you leave her alone with baby sitters so much?" she asked.

"Part of the reason is my work. The other," he paused again, now deep in thought trying to find the right words, "is that maybe I won't be around forever so maybe I want her to get used to looking after number one. Ever think of that Hemingway?" asked Dominic.

"Ever think that maybe she might just need her loving grandfather, I mean really need you to be there in her formative years, not just someone to pay the bills and keep her in line," argued Lisa.

"Sure are a lot of maybes. And while we're getting personal here, I hate to be picky, but why haven't you got yourself a guy in your life?" he asked.

"Because, Lieutenant, all the charming, single men in town are on the police force. And how do you know I don't?"

"Because if he's any kind of man you wouldn't be here with me right now."

"Please, you're not going to give me that ancient theory, a woman's place is in the home," she said.

"What's wrong with that? It worked for me some 35 years and would still if….." a silence came over Dominic.

"If what?" countered Lisa.

"Forget it," he said. "On second thought, you're probably one of those modern types who's got another woman stashed."

Lisa instantly flipped him the finger.

"Hum! Table for one," he replied.

A waitress stepped in between them to rally in Lisa's support. "Good for you, honey!" she said while scorning Dominic. "I'm with ya! Chauvinist pig. By the way beautiful," she said, "I get off around two if you're interested."

Lisa was at a complete loss for words. She certainly did not see that coming. She looked to Dominic to get his reaction, which was obvious. He had just gotten the call they both were waiting for.

"Yes, Dan, you got it! And the winner is?' he asked.

The Bonaventure Hotel was by now as world famous to L.A. as the Plaza was to New York City. Its marvelous circular design was a landmark for the modern world. Visitors from all nations flocked to her exquisite accommodations located directly in the center of the city just off the Hollywood freeway. Its lobby was one of the busiest in the world even with life's recessions coming and going. You just can't keep a good rich man down.

Derek James was by now thrilled when they called his name aloud. "Thank you, sir," said Derek taking the package while signing.

"Very good, sir," said the clerk.

Derek without a moment's delay headed for the nearest elevator, stopping down just one flight to the parking structure. He spotted Tyrone in his car. Here's the package, Tyrone," he said. "Joco said you would have further instructions."

The large thug pulled out his silenced Magnum and fired, killing Derek almost immediately. "No, that will definitely be all, my boy," answered Tyrone, as he tossed a note over the lifeless body.

Driving off he quickly dialed his boss, Joco, who immediately came on the speaker, "Yes?" he said.

"Sir, I have the package and that other problem has been solved." Pause. "Yes, sir, right away."

Derek James' apartment was deep in the heart of LA's newly remodeled lofts. It seemed instead of tearing down and out the old historic manufacturing plants, the creative minds had decided to upgrade and transform those turn of the last century sweatshops into artsy fartsy living quarters with hardly any inside walls for privacy and sharing a common freight elevator that dropped each and every tenant right at their actual doorstep.

Dominic was on the phone with his office. "I want a print team along with the CSI boys and girls dispatched to 1444 N. Alameda," pausing, "Yes, that's just down from Union Station."

"May I ask why we are here?" Lisa said.

"Because I want to know everybody this little prick has ever had in this giant trap. Anything that would tie him to something bigger."

"What prick?" she asked, "and what something bigger?"

"Small time young hustler, white, good-looking kid named Derek James."

"How did you get his name and address?"

"Dan said his DNA was all over the dead girl. Once we had that, there was no problem getting his address from the DMV. She wasn't killed here. Dan said his findings bore out the fact she was killed from a high fall. This building, however, has only four floors. It had to be a very high building to do that much damage, a hotel or swank apartment."

Dominic looked down at an end table and grabbed a book of matches. "This could be a club he frequents."

"What's your theory, Sherlock?" she asked.

"I think both Jenny Baxter and Parks' daughter met this guy, Derek, somewhere in one of those in punk or acid joints. Then they went onto better things. Pretty boy here is a pimp for some big drug dealer," said Dominic, showing Lisa Derek's picture ID. "And who knows, maybe we'll catch a break and pin this Amanda Parks party on my old fucking buddy, Joco. I'm sure his honor would be more than willing to cooperate in this case. After all, blood is thicker than money."

Once again Dominic's phone vibrated. He checked his caller ID. "Shit! It's Stillwell," he said to Lisa. "Yes Captain, yes sir. We're looking real good here. Just got a lead on the James kid." (Pause) "What's that? I know, Captain, we'll get right back on that. I just got a break in my case and felt I had to act on it." Dominic was by now holding his cell well away from his ear because there was way too much heat on the other end. "Yes sir, I know it sounds like, as you say, bull shit! But it's true," (Pause) "What's that, sir? Charley said what? He did. Great! Thanks boss for passing that on. Oh! One more thing, how did you know we'd be here?" he asked.

Awaiting his chief to give him some more insight, Dominic started laughing while he was repeating Stillwell's answer. "It's a secret and that's why you get the big bucks."

"What?" asked Lisa.

"There you go with that what again," said Dominic.

During all the dialog exchange with Stillwell there had been some activity back down on the street level, the kind of activity that involved a certain police car and its ignition. Two more of Joco's bungling mob were hooking up still another explosive trap.

Ever since that horrible night when the kids were mistakenly killed Dominic has had an automatic starting device installed within his computer key, allowing him to start the vehicle without being anywhere near it. Add to that his penchant for walking and talking while on his phone, he had noticed strangers milling about the car, one in particular concentrating on the driver's side. Putting it all together he concluded since no one in their fucking right minds would want to steal a cop car, they must be exercising foul play. So he did what any smart survivor would do. He took out his keys, held back and watched just long enough for those two illegal idiots to finish their chore with one still under the car and the other watching out nearby, leaning against the passenger door.

"I said it's my job. Are you still here, Lieutenant?" she asked.

"Charley remembered whose name he recognized the night he got shot."

"Who?" she asked.

"This guy is so connected it even scares me. Frank "the Skull" Pansine."

"Why do they call him the Skull?" she said.

"Don't ask. Pansine was the top dog that put that huge drug deal together with Joco and here's the best part, we don't even have to chase his ugly ass down. He got himself popped on some fucking parking tickets that all went to warrants. Right this moment he's cooling his heels as a guest of the county and is only about five minutes away," said Dominic, still staring out the window.

It looked to him this just might be an excellent opportunity to press a certain button. He whispered to himself, “Here’s another one for you and Chris, Jerry. Pay back is a bitch! Gentlemen start your engines!” He pressed down extra hard, bata-bing, bata-boom, a horrendous noise erupted, nearly driving Lisa right out of her premium Victoria’s Secret lingerie.

“What the hell was that?”

Still looking down at the street, Dominic answered, “Sounds like we might have to call a cab.”

Lisa and Dominic were both coming down the stairs from Derek James’ loft. As they both carefully passed by what was left of their car, hot flames continued to scrape the last of its metal frame, melting anything or anybody in its path. The neighborhood had come alive with looky-Lous, all trying their level best to get a peek at the loss of life.

“I wonder,” remarked Dominic, “if anybody bothered to call the police.”

“Lieutenant! How can you be so nonchalant about this! You just killed two men.”

“I only tried to start my car, and young lady, just as a side note, better them than us.”

A City Cab pulled up to the curb. “Lieutenant Pisa, I came just as fast as I could when I got your call.”

“Thanks Joey. Trying to get a cab in this town on short notice is about as sure a thing as the Dodgers moving back to Brooklyn! Huh, kid.”

“You got that right, sir. Where to?” he asked.

“County lockup.”

Joey, looked at young Lisa, “Men or women’s side?” he asked.

“Oh, she’s with me.”

CHAPTER 22

Minutes later they found themselves in a very different world, certainly foreign to anything Lisa was accustomed to. County Jail was noisy and over-crowded with prisoners and guards alike moving about in a kind of military cadence. The place was generally run down. The church-like pews that served its waiting visitors were a safe distance from the actual iron doors that led to the main jail section. Their paint had been chipping for quite a while and they reeked of body odor and cheap tobacco. One woman was passing her one dollar bills through the heavy bulletproof glass as if she were at the local bank for a deposit. The guard made note of the transaction then handed the bills to another deputy who washed the money.

"Why do they do that?" Lisa observed.

"So that there isn't a hint of drugs on the paper," answered Dominic. "Inmates sometimes roll up the bills and smoke them later if they were dipped in whatever first. It does happen."

The visiting section was also extremely crowded. Mothers were crying with the reality of just what a hell on earth for their beautiful children really looked like and they could just imagine what went on with lights out.

"You have got to be fucking nuts!" said Pansine to Dominic, "I got no names to name. I'm a dead man over here. On the outside maybe I got a shot but my guys aren't in here. That Moulie Joco's people practically run the joint." All the time Pansine was talking, he was preoccupied with Lisa.

"Lisa," said Dominic, "will you excuse us? Frank wants to speak to me in Italian." They talked for a few minutes more then Dominic got up and rejoined the young reporter.

"I'll tell you that man grosses me out," she said. "Did you see the way he looked at me? I felt naked."

"I sure did, kid. That's what put us over," said Dominic.

"I don't follow."

"He's a cinch to get 120 days. That's a long time for a guy of Pansine's appetites to go without, so I told him if he cooperated I could pull a few strings and get conjugal visits. Are you interested?" asked Dominic.

"I think he's right about one thing, you are fucking nuts," said Lisa.

"Actually, I told him if he didn't give me some answers I'd pass the word out he did anyway. Ha!"

"So what was the bottom line?" asked Lisa.

"He gave me what he had on Joco's last known address. Now I'll have search warrants generated, along with a team within the hour. Until then we go slumming."

Dominic's police dispatcher was coming through loud and clear on Joey's radio frequency as Dominic and Lisa reached the unusual cab. "One-700, see the team, Park Manor. We have a confirmed 187. Respond."

Dominic looked to Lisa while he grabbed the receiver from Joey.

"Affirmative, will respond. You know it Joey" asked Dominic.

"Copy that Lieutenant, gotcha covered."

“Looks like our guy has been busy,” said Dominic.

“A little too busy for my tastes,” she said.

“Relax, Lisa. He’s only after good-looking pros, not amateurs.”

“I’ll take that as a compliment, Lieutenant, I think. One thing more, how come Joey here knows so much about you and your business? He even has a police radio.”

“I know, I got it for him. You see, Joey helps me out every now and then when I lose my wheels or on occasion he even drives me home from certain establishments which will remain nameless.”

Chet Higgins was talking with the doorman and the building manager at the crime scene just as our trio drove up.

“Just what I told the uniformed officer. Must I go there again?”

“Yes! Tell me! He might just get it wrong.”

The doorman pointed to the body, “I let her and a companion out of his limousine around 9 p.m. They kissed, exchanged a few words. He got back in and drove off and she went inside.”

“Then what happened?”

“About an hour or so later I went inside to relieve myself.”

“To what?” asked Chet.

“To wring it out! Okay? And that’s when I thought I saw something through the automatic doors that lead past the pool area where our new bungalows are. I walked down that same path she would of took. The closer I got to what I thought I saw, the more I realized this was a dead body. She was just as she is now, half in and half out of the shrubs."

"You didn't hear anything suspicious?"

"No sir. What a horrible thing. She seemed like such a nice kid, too," the doorman said.

"Not that nice. She was working here," said Dominic.

"She was a human being and now she's dead."

"Bravo! I agree," said Lisa.

"You're not here to agree or disagree. Just print the facts, no editorializing if you don't mind," Dominic replied.

"Well of all the narrow-minded (pause), I think if these victims were." (Searching)

"Whores?" he said.

"Escorts," she said, "you might find it in that pump you generously call a heart to catch this beast a little sooner."

"Am I to understand you are from the press? Oh my, could we possibly keep the Manor out of the papers?" said the manager, who had just been called in to handle things. "This kind of publicity would be most damaging."

"Not half as damaging if I catch anyone else residing here who is selling anything without a license. Get my meaning?" he asked. "Anybody else see or hear anything?" asked Dominic.

"So far we drew a blank."

Dominic leaned down for a closer look at the body. Her neck was broken, snapped like a twig. "Just like the others. A powerful person did this. She was no lightweight, 5 feet 11 inches tall and135 pounds, I make it."

Dominic began placing his arms on Lisa's shoulders. "I figure it happened like this. Lisa, pretend you're the whore. Just relax, walk back over to the entrance and I'll give you the go ahead."

Lisa agreed reluctantly. Dominic took her through the motions by the numbers. "One," He yelled, waving her on. "You say goodnight outside in the circular drive up. George here," referring to the doorman.

"Charles, sir. My name is Charles."

"Okay, Charlie here lets you in. you walk straight past him through the double sliding glass doors and out into the pool area.

"Two: You've got your eyes well down in your expensive handbag trying to find your keys in that sea of shit you call a purse."

Lisa looked up quickly in disgust.

"Just continue to look down.

"Three: Suddenly you stop. Why? Because you got interrupted by a voice from anywhere. It's not a familiar voice but you think if it's here in this full security building it must be safe. There's always a risk you tell yourself, but one worth taking if the price is right. Besides the night is young, so you press on. The voice continues to lure you."

"So lure me," said Lisa.

Pisa by this time was becoming annoyed. "Will you please! Just lure. She kept coming towards him and just when you think you have scored your next rich benefactor, the killer reaches out through those bushes and powerfully envelopes your mouth and throat with his giant hands, picking up your more than average frame in the process and snapping your beautiful neck."

"That would account for the fact there was no screaming," said Chet.

"Pretty scary," said Lisa.

Chet motioned for the other team members. "Comb the area kids for footprints. We had some early rain yesterday. I want a cast of any feet you might find. A guy this big and strong will have to weigh at least 200 pounds. That makes a big dent in soft soil. Tear out those shrubs if you have to. This prick has killed for the last time."

"Carry on Mr. Higgins, Ms. Powers and I have a few more stops to make," said Dominic.

CHAPTER 23

Modeling agencies were as plentiful in the greater Los Angeles area as pizza parlors were in Little Italy. Some, I had little doubt, were legitimately trying to promote all their clients into whatever world, be it fashion, runway, or motion pictures. Whenever anyone, boy or girl, told me they were models, I immediately conjured up all those dirty pictures. Perhaps that just might be my wishful thinking at work.

The Monica Beale Agency certainly would fit within that mental mold. Their very exclusive suite of offices and headquarters worldwide were located deep in the heart of Wilshire Blvd. just blocks away from the internationally known Rodeo Drive and its priceless store fronts.

Two young detectives had just entered and announced themselves.

"Mrs. Beale will be right with you, Sargent," said the receptionist, pausing as she studied the good looking young man. "You don't look like a police officer, you look more like one of our own male models."

"No thanks, I work with my clothes on," said Murtaugh very uncomfortably. "Not all cops wear a mustache, a cheap suit and wing tips."

"That's it!" she said. "You kinda remind me of the guy I bought my used BMW from. You could pass for brothers."

"I'm thrilled," he said. "You do any modeling yourself?"

"Sorry," she answered, "I just have office skills."

"May I be of service to you gentleman? I'm Monica Beale. I own this establishment," she said firmly, extending her beautiful hand in earnest.

"Yes Ma'am, we're hoping you can shed some light," said Sgt. Murtaugh, digging for the murder victim's photos he had jammed deep in his coat pocket.

"I don't understand," she replied.

"Do you recognize any of these young ladies?" he asked.

Mrs. Beale studied each and every photo carefully, "No I can't say I do. They are not under contract to my agency. Why, may I ask?"

"They were all brutally murdered. This one," he pointed out, "was killed less than five hours ago."

"That's horrible. But why do you think I would have known them?" she asked.

"Because you also, I'm told, run a very high-end escort agency as well. All these ladies here have records for escorting."

"Careful Sargent, you are on uneasy ground. I know some pretty influential judges in this town who just might have your badge," she countered.

"I'm sure you do, I know a few myself, one or two well enough to pester at any hour and come back here with a warrant and go through those modeling files."

"What is it you want?" she asked, calming down.

“I want you to call me at this number,” handing her his card. “My direct line is there as well. You can reach me immediately. Call the minute one of your girls is missing for any reason or if a client, no matter whom, seems just a bit left of center. Anything out of the ordinary, no matter what.”

“As you wish, Officer Murtaugh,” said Mrs. Beale, reading his card.

The two officers had barely left the building when the phone rang.

“Good evening, Beale Modeling,” answered the receptionist.

“And a good evening to you, young lady,” said a raspy voice on the other end of the call. “I’m new in town and I’d be remiss if I left without seeing the extreme beauty that your extraordinary city welcomes. Could you perhaps recommend someone who would help me fulfill that wish?” he asked.

“I don’t understand. We run a strict modeling agency. How did you hear about us?” she asked the unusual voice.

“Dr. Farnsworth suggested I call.”

“Farnsworth?” she repeated while searching her computer files.

“That’s him,” he said quickly.

“Oh yes, the doctor has been with us for quite some time. When would you like someone available?” she asked.

“Tonight would be splendid! Is that a problem?” he asked.

"Well it is getting rather late in the day. I'll see what we can do since you know the doctor."

"I'm stopping at the Mar-Mount not too far from you."

"I know it. Give me your name and room number and I'll get back."

"Marvelous," he said slowly. "That's Ralph Turner, as in Ted. Room 245, and I'd like to take a moment to thank you for your assistance. You've been extremely helpful and I'll be sure to mention this to the good doctor."

"Thank you," said the naïve receptionist. "You'll hear from us."

The raspy, uneasy voice hung up the phone. He tucked a black book of numbers he had into his desk drawer, pushing the crowded items about to make room, exposing what looked to be a badge and a gun, a 40-caliber Glock to be exact.

CHAPTER 24

Dominic and Lisa approached the bouncer. He was the one who decided yes you do or no you do not get to enter that private den, of you name it. They were at the Joy Box which turned out to be the beginning of the end for two young, beautiful, misguided teens.

"Excuse me folks," said the more than a fair hand, young, burly and muscular usher. "I'll have to check your IDs."

"You're kidding," said Lisa, "we're both over 21."

"Yeah, I can see that! You're marginal but this guy," referring to Dominic, "has to be older than my father. Everyone should be between 18 and 25, plus be a member or know someone."

"I know the mayor," said Dominic, displaying his badge. "I'll be sure and pass on how cooperative you were, young man."

"Sorry Lieutenant," said the boy, checking his ID. "I can't be too careful. A lot of old guys have a thing for young girls."

"Well I have a thing for middle-aged girls. You got any aunts that would like a mature Italian type fellow?"

"I can make some calls," said the bouncer grinning.

"No thanks. While I got you here, ever see this kid?"

The bouncer was glancing at Derek James' picture. "Sure, he's in and out all the time. Practically lives here! Why?"

"He's part of an ongoing murder investigation."

"Fuck," said the boy," you might check with the bartender inside. Stuart's his name. He's a three dollar bill but knows everybody."

A tall, handsome, young man with more than a hint of effeminateness greeted them. "Can I help you?" he asked.

"Oh!" said Dominic producing his badge, "I'm sure you can."

"It's like that is it?" Stuart asked.

"It's like that," answered Dominic pulling out the matchbook.

"If you need a light Lieutenant, we've got hundreds and you can smoke on the patio."

"I got these from Derek James."

"What's a Derek James?" asked Stuart sarcastically.

Dominic seemed to ignore Stuart's disrespect, he grabbed Lisa's purse and emptied its contents onto the bar, very much to her surprise. "Take a look, kid!" said Dominic losing his patience. "Ever see any of these three in here?" he asked, pointing to Derek's license and the pictures he took off the Baxter girl's computer.

"Must be bad lighting," said Stuart.

Dominic moved behind the bar directly in front of him, grabbing the boy's crotch. "You know, Stuart, I would hate like hell to ruin your evening but I can't have you ruining mine either! So let's start over," said Dominic squeezing his balls, "and see just how many high notes you can hit!"

"Come to think of it," said Stuart with a definite attitude adjustment, "those girls do look a bit familiar."

"And when did you last see them?" asked Dominic.

"They left with him," answered Stuart in extreme pain, pointing to Derek's ID. "That's him all right. Just your average, drop-dead gorgeous young man!" said Stuart, who is near tears.

"A real stand out! Ladies man, eh?" said Dominic.

"Unfortunately," said Stuart.

"And I'll just bet you know where they went, right kid?"

"I don't know, man! Honest."

"Really, Stuart, I'm disappointed. We had such a good beginning here," said Dominic, increasing his grip.

"Party! They went off to some party!"

Lisa was standing there observing this brutality. However, she had learned not to butt in when it came to so called police work.

"Okay," asked Dominic, "and where would you say that party took place?

"Some big shot's," grimaced Stuart.

"Now here's the climax! A name, Stuart, now would be a good time for a name, son!"

"All I know is this guy is black. Even if I knew his name, I'd be dead in 24 hours if I told you. Please! Enough."

“My! My! He must be a real bad man. Well, I’ll tell you, Stuart, we’ve hit enough notes for one night. You done good,” said Dominic flipping the boy a crisp, freshly printed fifty dollar bill. “Here. Buy yourself a strong athletic cup because if you’re thinking about giving anybody a heads up after we leave, forget it, or I will be back. Capiche?”

“Yes, sir,” said the frightened boy.

“You know, Pisa, you never cease to amaze me. You and your twisted bedside manner,” Lisa remarked as they were leaving the private bar.

“Well,” said Dominic, “you get much more with a gun and a kind word than you do with just a kind word. Besides I’ll lay odds he secretly loved every minute of it.”

CHAPTER 25

There were few, if any, spots left over from Hollywood's glorious past. You could probably count them all on one hand. Two equally famous came to mind simply because not only were the buildings still standing but they were both doing a thriving business as usual, Musso and Frank's Restaurant and Bar centered on Hollywood Blvd. and the always busy and beautiful Old English style Chateau Marmount, one block off Sunset Blvd. This classy hideaway was barely visible from the street, a perfect spot for a rich clandestine meeting, be it two current personality flavors of the month around town or just a highly priced male or female lover looking to pad their bank balance compliments of some visiting Jon.

Gorgeous Debby Daniels certainly fit the female pattern there at the Chateau that night. At first sight one would never mistake her innocent manner and courtly carriage for one of Monica Beale's ladies of the night. Nothing cheap about this gal, everything about her from head to toe was choice, prime cut and she even had a brain. What a bonus. She had graduated with honors from some Eastern Ivy league school of business. Smart about her money too, she had invested wisely, if that were even possible in today's ever plunging profit columns. For quite some time her figures bore out the strong possibility she could retire shortly with a sizable financial nest egg. Debby was only maybe twenty-seven at most, kept her body in solid shape with a helpful personal trainer, lifted weights daily and maintained a rigid self defense regimen.

Her cell phone rang with an unknown display, perfectly normal for a girl in her line of work. She answered, "Yes, this is Debby."

"Hi, this is Ralph. I'm the one Monica Beale recommended. Are you here in the lobby?" the stranger asked.

"I'm already in the elevator."

"Splendid, room 245," said the foggy voice.

"How is it you know Monica?" she asked.

"You and I have a mutual friend, Dr. Marc Farnsworth, the surgeon."

"I'm impressed," she answered. "If you're half the man he was we'll get along beautifully."

The room door was slightly ajar as Debby arrived and the lights were once again low key.

"Hello," said Debby pushing the door open just wide enough, allowing for her stunning and spectacular figure. "Are you still in here?" she asked, walking well into the room.

"Right behind you, bitch!" mumbled the killer, grabbing her around the neck and once again forcibly picking her up. But before he could brutally crack her neck and spine, he was in for the surprise of his sick, predatory life. Debbie slammed her right arm directly downward behind her into his groin. He immediately released his grip, grabbing his privates while doubling over in extreme pain.

Once freed from his lock she drove her shapely knee upwards into his chin, catching her assailant once again off guard and placing him onto his shocked backside out into the hall. He was wearing a mask of some sort, distorting his features. With a coupe-de-grace, as the

French executioners called it, she firmly kicked him a couple more times in the head into unconsciousness for good measure.

She immediately retreated as fast as those lovely legs would carry her back to the elevator, down to the lobby and out into a busy mid evening crowd. She hit her Beale Agency logged number. It rang, they answered. "Beale Modeling Agency, Loraine speaking. How can I help you?" she asked in earnest.

"By not hooking me up with some fucking head case, you stupid twit!" said Debby in violent anger.

"Take it easy. Is that you, Ms. Daniels?" she asked.

"You bet your lame brain it is."

"Calm down and tell me what this is all about," said the receptionist.

"That crazy friend of Dr. Farnsworth you booked me with. The son-of-a-bitch tried to kill me!"

"Why didn't you call the police, Debby?"

"That's a joke. What do I tell them? I was in his room, a perfect stranger, having tea and we had this little disagreement. Besides there were no witnesses and it would be his word against mine, sweetheart!" I have been able to survive these past years by keeping a low profile. I've never been popped."

"This gets worse," said the receptionist. "You're not the first working girl who has been attacked recently. You're just the first one that got away!"

"Fuck! Are you telling me there's a serial killer on the loose?"

"Six girls dead so far. You're the only one from our book," said Loraine.

"How is it you know so much about this?" Debby asked.

"There were two police officers from homicide in today."

"Today!" yelled Debby. "And you called me anyway?"

"He said he was new in town, a friend of Dr. Farnsworth. The doctor always enjoyed you so very much I figured it was a match made in….."

"Hell!" Debby interrupted. "Now listen to me carefully. Call those cops right back, but you never heard of me. Make up a story you got an anonymous tip an hour ago. A freelance whore was attacked by some nut wearing a Halloween mask in room 245 – Chateau Marmount. She fought him off and was able to get away. Got it? Now don't fuck this up, Loraine. If they hurry, they just might still catch his big, sorry ass down and out in the hallway. You tell Monica this is one she owes me. I'm going to take a little trip. Don't call me, I'll call you!"

The Beale Modeling Agency hadn't had this much heat since the fire of 2005. Chet Higgins and his crack team were back checking Monica's files for any clients who might have shared any common denominators with the crazy bastard that seemed to kill with untimely precision.

"Loraine, right?" asked Murtaugh.

"Yes, officer," she answered.

"You told one of our guys that you got an unknown call telling you about an alleged attack on some girl over at the Marmount in Hollywood?"

"Correct! About ten minutes before I called you. The girl said if you hurried you might catch him. She bragged about leaving him unconscious just outside the room."

"We already checked that out. We sent two guys. They found nothing outside that room number or inside that would seem there was anyone there, let alone a physical skirmish. The desk told them no one had booked that room for tonight."

Dominic and Lisa had just entered and were met by Chet, who introduced everyone. Chet was bringing Dominic up to speed off to one side.

"Who was it who called Miss Loraine here?" asked Chet.

"She didn't say, Boss," said Officer Rielly still sifting through the files while marveling at all the extreme beauty. "Now, Lorraine, did you recognize the voice at all?" asked Chet, "And did the caller say she knew the girl that was attacked? I mean, did the alleged victim tell her?"

"No and no," answered the frightened girl.

"Well that's hell of a lot of information, young lady, from someone you don't know about a girl she doesn't know.

"I've got a question," said Dominic. "Why would that mystery voice even bother to call here about some whore and her business?"

"You do run a legitimate agency here, right Monica?" Mrs. Beale asked Dominic.

"I do Lieutenant."

"Bull shit! This whole thing about that anonymous call, it all stinks, or in today's vernacular, it sucks. And pardon the pun ladies," said Dominic, "you want to know what I think? Well, I'll tell you anyway. My theory is Loraine knew the caller because she's in your trick book cross-referenced with certain men who don't mind spending money on something they can no longer get for free. You know, lady, yo may not drive a pink Cadillac, wear loud outfits and a tacky fedora but for my money you're still a pimp. Now before you go off defending yourself and your operation we can play this one of two ways. We can take this down to the station and all sweat or you can cooperate. What's it going to be?"

Monica Beale is in deep thought. "Tell him, Loraine, everything."

"Yes, ma'am," she answered. "Debby Daniels was the girl that called. She went to the Marmount and was attacked but was able to get away safely."

"How did she manage that? This guy is big, strong and extremely motivated," asked Dominic.

"She studies martial arts and is in great shape," Loraine said.

"A great looking girl with a beautiful body and the ability to protect it," said Dominic. One in a million. Did you set up that sparring match?" he asked.

"Yes sir," she answered. "The stranger called up and said he was a friend of another client, Dr. Farnsworth, Marc Farnsworth, the surgeon."

"I'm impressed," said Chet. "Check that out," he said to Murtaugh.

"I want a name and address ASAP on this Debby. Pick her up, maybe we'll catch a break and he might try for a rematch," adds Dominic.

"I'm going outside for a nail."

Chet followed him out. "That shit is going to kill you, Pap," referring to the cigarettes.

"Everybody dies. How many times you had your ass shot at, not including the Army?" asked Dominic.

"You got a point, Paison. You know, Pap, I thought I knew all there was to homicide investigation and was good at it, but this bird has me stumped."

"You are a great cop, Chet Higgins. Never, ever lose sight of that. And you drink pretty good too. Old school."

"It's almost like he's laughing at us!" said Chet. "Like he knows just what our next move will be."

"Suppose he does?" asked Dominic taking one of his deep drags.

"What?" answered Chet with a question.

"Let's run down what we know about this prick. He's a big, strong guy who hates women or prostitutes for sure. Maybe uses women. He has some knowledge of martial arts. He obviously knows connected people, pimps, madams, etc. and well enough to have them all do his bidding. Where does he get all his clout? He's either very rich and buys them off or he uses intimidation and who, my good friend, uses that little chestnut?" asked Dominic.

"Mob. You think he's a wise guy?"

"Maybe. That's a possibility," said Dominic. "But who else uses intimidation?"

"We do!" they both chimed in.

"A rogue cop is the killer?" shouted Chet.

"Maybe! Not a real officer. Somehow I don't buy him on the force. How about a security guy? They have access. Let's check all the hotels where those girls were killed. Find out whether they have in-house dicks or use an outside vendor. If we get a break there then we tap their computors for our friend. He shouldn't be too hard to find. The shit always floats to the top."

"Pisa, you're fucking brilliant," said Chet.

"Yeah, not bad," said Dominic.

Murtaugh ran up to them looking just like the cat that swallowed the mouse.

"Did you check out that Debby Daniels lead?" asked Chet.

"Yes, sir. She's history! I mean long gone to wherever. Her roommate said she came home long enough to throw a few things in a large Gucci and split. May I say something, sir?" Murtaugh asked.

"Okay, let's have it, but be brief."

"Well, this man we're after knows too much about everything, especially our end. I feel he's close to one of us, maybe even," he hesitates.

"Go on son," said Chet, "don't stop now."

"Well this is gonna sound pretty shaky, maybe even stupid, but maybe he's a cop or close to it."

"Interesting theory, son! Don't you think, Chet?" asked Dominic.

"Very, Pap."

"I figured you'd think that, so I pursued it. I cross-checked all the hotels and came up with a winner, Denton Systems."

“Come again?” asked Chet.

“They’re the security experts for most of the high dollar hotels in LA and Holly-weird including the ones where the murders were committed. Shall I continue?”

“Please do, son,” said Dominic.

“I took what we have on the killer, you know size, stronger than most, a rough-talking voice, scratchy, and I had them run it through their computer files. It came up with three possibilities, one’s a standout.”

“Let’s hear it!” ordered Chet.

“Simon Taggart. Fifteen year Army Ranger with two tours in Iraq specializing in guerilla tactics and expert weaponry. Over thirty personal kills, mostly by hand. And this is especially interesting, he was mustered out on a medical. He caught some shrapnel in his throat.”

“Well, you got everything else on this guy. How about an address?”

Murtaugh handed Dominic everything, “14532 Saticoy. Hell! That’s way out in the valley,” read Dominic. “Call North Hollywood division, have them suit up and meet us at that address pronto. SWAT if they got one. We need all the help we can get if we’re going to get Taggart, dead or alive, that’s the way I see this played out. You boys okay with that?”

“I just want to say great work, kid,” said Chet to his officer. “Only next time share the gold. One thing more, let’s proceed with extreme caution. This man is not only highly dangerous but he is very intelligent. He’s beat us at every turn. Pap, you got anything to add?” asked Chet.

“Just this, we can’t have any legal slip ups or some white-haired prick on a bench is gonna give him a walk.”

"I'd like to say something," said Lisa, joining the officers, while waving off once again Dominic's smoke. "I think this detective's a credit to his badge for this brilliant piece of police work."

"That's Dan Murtaugh, Ms. Powers, in case you might want to write anything down," said Dominic grinning. "Let's roll."

CHAPTER 26

The 14500 block on Satiloy was for the most part strictly CI, very commercial. Taggart's place looked to be an old sweat shop. The building had to be at least 85 years old.

When the San Fernando Valley region was all orange groves, perhaps his place might have been a packaging plant or where they manufactured orange juice. What our killer has put there since he has had residency, one could just imagine. Several units were strategically spotted. Within minutes the aging concrete and brick building was surrounded with no possible way out. Chet Higgins, complete with pump-action shotgun, flack vest and radio was in full command.

"Well, Paison," he said, "here we go again."

"I kinda get the realization lately like some of our middle-aged movie heroes that I'm getting a bit long in the tooth for this kind of shit," said Dominic. "Taggart couldn't be this milk-toast bank teller type, he's got to be fucking Rambo and built like a tree."

"No matter what way we go, it's gonna get nasty before it gets good," said Chet picking up his bullhorn. "Simon Taggart! This is Lieutenant Chet Higgins, Los Angeles Police Department, Hollywood Homicide Division. You are completely surrounded. Come out with your hands clasped over your head. You've got exactly ten minutes to comply!"

"Well," said Dominic, "there goes the element of surprise."

"Stillwell's right on," replied Chet. "You are a smart ass."

"You know, Chet, what they say about us New Yorkers, we're just like everybody else only a little more so."

Lisa Powers was wedged in between Dominic and young Murtaugh. She was beginning to notice the ruggedly handsome officer.

"When the shooting starts, Ms. Powers, please keep your head down and try not to move."

"You won't get any argument from me, officer. It is Dan, right?"

"Yes, ma'am," he answered.

Taggart's time was up. Chet traded his air horn for a hand radio. He pressed its lever. "This is Higgins to SWAT commanders. I want a barrage of tear gas. Aim for the bottom floor first, then work your way up, counting down from 5, 4, 3, 2, 1, commence firing."

The building was hit from all sides. At least 40 rounds made their mark.

"Cease fire!" yelled Chet.

A few more minutes went by. Still nothing.

"This is fucked," Chet said to Murtaugh. "Are you sure Taggart is even in there?"

"Affirmative, sir. A night watchman across the street spotted him going in about an hour ago."

"What's your take on this, Pap?"

"Well," answered Dominic, "one thing is for certain. It doesn't look like he's coming out, so if we want his ass we got to go in there and take it."

Chet rested a beat to digest what his idol had said. "SWAT commanders, Higgins again. We are going in. Synchronize the time. We'll deploy at exactly 21.5, come in from all sides. Don't take any unnecessary chances. I repeat the suspect is extremely dangerous. Time ticked off, 21.3, 21.4 and finally 21.5. The scene once again exploded with gunfire. Chet, Dominic and Murtaugh all made for Taggart's front door with SWAT teams everywhere leading the way. Four men carrying a battering bar rounded a corner and charged the entrance, tearing it to pieces, followed by countless police shadows armed with semiautomatics, ripping everything in their path. They couldn't lose. They had it all, manpower and firepower, an unbeatable combination, or so it would seem. But Simon Taggart, however, had other ideas.

He was systematically filtering his way back through the pack, hugging the walls. He was dressed as one of their own, flack suit, gas mask, radio and all, mounting casualties along his way.

Higgins and his well-trained team had certainly met their match this night. Once deep into Taggart's fort a frightening discovery was made. C-4 plastic explosives had been strategically placed throughout the bulletproof structure in order to execute his plan to make his home a lasting shrine for some fifty brave men. He needed only to clear the building then trigger electronically the deadly device by hitting a send number on his cell phone.

Suddenly he saw Lisa, who just happened to be blocking his final escape route. He grabbed the unsuspecting reporter.

"Hey! What the hell gives?" yelled Lisa. The bad guy is in there.

“Shut the fuck up, bitch!” said the raspy-voiced killer. “I have to make an important phone call.”

He was about to dial when a brilliant shot entered directly through Taggart’s mask, exploding his head and killing him instantly.

Lisa fainted dead away at the sight. When she finally came around, young Dan Murtaugh was directly over her.

“I’m sorry if I frightened you, Ms. Powers. It had to be done. He would have brought down that entire warehouse on all those men and notched you permanently in the company of those other unfortunate beauties.”

“I guess I should say thanks, Officer Murtaugh.”

“Dan, remember. I was just doing my job.”

“How many we lose?” asked Chet.

“Not as many as we could have it weren’t for this kid,” answered Dominic pointing to Murtaugh.

“Well, it’s time for us older folks to head home. I’ll call Stillwell, Chet, and give him the good news. Ms. Powers shall we away?”

“You don’t have to ask twice! What a story. Nobody down at WKLT is going to believe the day I’ve had,” Lisa said.

CHAPTER 27

Lisa and Dominic both adjourned to their brand new, state-of-the-art police car sent to them compliments of Captain Stillwell.

"This is beautiful," said Lisa, "and I never thought I'd ever say that about any professional city ride."

"I'll second that thought, young lady," replied Dominic. "This has everything possible. Its got the solid looks of heavy armor with all the comforts of a priceless Cadillac and will probably get three more miles to the gallon than Hitler's Mercedes."

Dominic was examining the car's new radio system. "Everything looked to be hands off, just a button here and there on the steering column, some voice activated. Let's see if we can wake the old man. One-700 calling. Do you copy?"

"Yes, Dominic. Do we have good news or bad?" Sue asked.

"It's a surprise! Patch me through will you honey? You might want to step out for a minute or hold your ears," said Dominic to Lisa. "This might get a little ugly."

"Everything I've been through so far as a guest of the city has prepared me, you better believe it, for whatever dialogue that would spill out from your boss. It won't even make a crack in my new-found thick shell."

"Stillwell here."

"Did I wake you Chief?" asked Dominic.

"Nonsense. How could I in good conscious rest worth a damn with you and the rest of the boys at risk?"

"Well now," said Dominic, "you can relax. Taggart has gone away for good. Dan Murtaugh did the honors just as that crazy bastard was about to kill us all with the C-4 explosives he had packed into every orifice in that concrete tomb. However sir, we do have a few of our own letters to write. That's always at times a harsh reality," said Stilwell. "We do our absolute best when our ass is on the line and then pray to God it's enough. Amen!" said Dominic. "So Captain, how's about me and my lady reporter jumping back on my case come Monday?"

"My God!" replied Stillwell, "you mean you didn't get the word? They found that kid Derek James tonight in the lower parking structure at the Bonaventure Hotel with a bullet screwed into his brain. And they were thoughtful enough to leave you a note!"

"How sweet," replied Dominic sarcastically. "Read it, will you boss?"

"It says only, 'Pisa! Don't get too close and stay in your own backyard.' It's not signed."

"No need Captain. This has Joco Martinez written all over it! This is just his latest bouquet. Over and out, Captain."

"Sounds like a bad break for the good guys," said Lisa.

Dominic was racking his tired brain. "I wonder what the hell he meant by staying in my own backyard." He repeated the phrase over and over until finally a light went on. He at last caught its true meaning and intent. "Oh my God! No! Please dear God not my little Maria!" he yelled.

He headed off towards his place just as fast and as loud as his new ride could carry them.

Dominic had screeched the car up to his place, stepped up to the busted and smashed security entrance, drew his weapon and proceeded down the darkened hall toward his apartment.

"Maria! Are you there, baby? It's Papa." No answer. "Maria! Answer me," he snapped. "Mrs. Cooper," he yelled. Still no answer. Not a sound.

He continued past Mrs. Cooper's door to his, which was wide open. He motioned back to Lisa Powers to stay absolutely still. The he burled his way into his living room, only to discover the bludgeoned and very dead baby sitter. He was by now to the point of tears, dreading the thought of what he might find next.

Well inside Maria's bedroom he discovered a note crudely printed with lipstick on the young child's dressing mirror. "Pig," it said. "If you don't want your granddaughter to end up like the rest of your family come to the end of Pier Ave., Berth 25 tonight! Alone. If I even smell backup she's dead!"

He made his way back to his car, breezed by a frightened Lady Anchor, burning brand new rubber while knocking over half the trash cans in the immediate neighborhood.

Lisa was in shock as she witnessed Dominic's uncompromising stare and resolve she had seen twice before when he was truly in control and taking things into his own hands. She called 911 on her cell. God willing Dominic would get there in time to save this little girl she too had grown extremely fond of.

Dominic had indeed arrived. He looked up and with the aid of his police mag-light was able to confirm the correct address. Pier Ave., Berth 25. It was a small warehouse located directly on the Long Beach docks.

Dominic was moving cautiously about with his light in one hand and his solemn 38 in the other, when suddenly a voice from nowhere ordered, "Lose the hardware, Dominic. No girl, no gun."

"Only my close friends call me by my first name, asshole! You can call me Lieutenant Sir."

"Shine that light over here Wop!" replied Joco.

Dominic complied, exposing Joco accompanied by his man, Tyrone, and an unconscious Maria.

"Tyrone, won't you convince this Lieutenant Sir to give it up."

Tyrone eagerly placed the 44-Magnum handgun he was gripping in his massive hand to the base of Maria's brain. Dominic reacted immediately, tossing over his piece.

"Good choice! Now then, do exactly as I say and maybe this little shit will have a future. Get down on your knees and place your fucking hands behind your head."

Dominic cooperated fully.

"Now I just want to say a few things to you. We haven't got a whole lot of time here. Why me? Back in New York always you on my ass! I could get to anybody or if I couldn't the real big bad boys could. You never got the picture, you guinea cowboy, you just kept on coming, not even after your son and daughter-in-law bought it. The only fucking thing in this world you give a good goddamn about is at my mother fucking feet. I want to hear you beg. Beg for her life just once and crawl."

"Don't hurt her, please! She's got nothing to do with all this. It's me you want. Spare her."

"You fucking pigs are all weak when it comes right down to it! No balls. I thought the one thing they taught you pricks in blue was never to give up your weapon!" yelled Joco, spitting at Dominic. "Tyrone," he continued, "will you please put our officer friend here out of his obvious misery?"

Tyrone removed his powerful piece from Maria's head and re-aimed it directly at her grandfather. Simultaneously Dominic reacted with almost cat-like reflexes, tossing a razor-sharp knife he had hidden in his coat collar directly into the throat of his assailant. While Tyrone desperately struggled for his last breaths, Joco receded back once again into the darkness.

Dominic picked up his 38 and checked his granddaughter, who was miraculously void of physical harm. "Maria! Maria! Baby, you all right?" he asked tightly holding his precious heir close to him.

"Damn!" said Maria, coming around. "I must have passed out."

"You watch your mouth young lady!"

"Grandpa, they killed Mrs. Cooper."

"I know, sweetheart."

Maria by this time had spotted the very dead bodyguard, still bleeding out because part of Dominic's blade had cut deep into a main artery. She reacted violently with a scream and passed out for a second time. Before

Dominic could revive her Lisa roared up with a large police posse and her own personal video guy.

"You stay with the ladies boys," ordered Dominic, "I have some unfinished business." Off he went in his hot pursuit with all lights green for the kill.

Joco had boarded a nearby vessel. It had the looks of a beached party cruiser. The only sounds heard this night aboard her pitching decks were those of two men and their dangerous echoes. Then a complete silence, not even a breath. This continued for what seemed like an eternity. Finally Dominic decided to press on, only to trip over some nearby cable of sorts. Dropping his gun onto the deck and losing his sense of balance, he fell forward into a black hole which seemed to be an empty swimming pool.

Joco was holding up Dominic's gun. "Looking for this!" he grinned, while opening fire.

Dominic was moving from side to side in the empty tank hoping to ward off Joco's attack. Only the flash from the police revolver was visible.

"I'm lovin life," Joco said, squeezing off two more of Dominic's valuable rounds without much luck. "Pretty cute trick back there. Caught my boy, Tyrone, napping but good. Never knew a white boy to be so good with a shiv. Sure you don't have a sister somewhere down that guinea line?" Joco, almost out of ammo had managed to find light bright enough to fill his sights. Finally they both had come face to face but certainly not on even ground. Joco was about to jerk off the kill shot. Dominic was ready to face whatever. He could see Joco's evil grin.

"Looks like your luck just ran out old boy," said Joco.

Suddenly there was a huge thud as Joco Martinez's lifeless body fell forward into the pool at Dominic's feet, revealing none other than Judge Manville Parks holding what appeared to be a harpoon gun.

"You're the last guy I ever expected to save my ass."

"My little girl," he mumbled, "she will never be the same, never!"

"Well your Honor," answered Dominic, climbing out of the pool, "shit happens!"

The scene became merged with countless policemen pouring in on all sides, their sparkling on and off red party hats were visible everywhere. Lisa stared down into the by now well lit murder scene. She saw Joco's remains. "Is that the man you have been hunting?" she asked.

"That's him, or what's left."

"Well can I tell my viewers that you have finally got them all?"

"That wouldn't be quite accurate, Ms. Powers. You see tonight I finally got a much needed hand from the legal community." Two officers were bringing Judge Parks forward already in handcuffs. "Say hello to the fella that really got our boy down there."

She was shocked to see his Honor in such a fix. "I'm so sorry, Judge," she said.

"I'm not, young lady," he replied as he was led off.

"Maria's out front with a police woman," said Lisa.

"Thanks! Now let's go fetch that beautiful little Italian blessing."

Maria spotted her patriarch through the crowd and ran into his arms. “Grandpa, I heard all those loud shots. I was so scared! I didn’t want you to die!”

Dominic leaned down, picked her up, and gave her a wink and a kiss. “I’m not going anywhere for quite a while, honey. What you say we get the hell out of here!”

“Papa, watch your mouth!”

He looked into her eyes for a brief moment. “You do have a point,” and looking over to Lisa Powers he repeated, “She definitely does have a point. Don’t you think so, Partner?” he asked Lisa.

Lisa Powers grinned, knowing full well she had at last earned her stripes.

CPSIA information can be obtained at www.ICGtesting.com
Printed in the USA
LVOW072026050713

341623LV00022B/742/P

9 781589 096929